CAPPUCCINO CRIMINAL

A Killer Coffee Mystery

Book Twelve

BY
TONYA KAPPES

TONYA KAPPES
WEEKLY NEWSLETTER

Want a behind-the-scenes journey of me as a writer?
The ups and downs, new deals, book sales, giveaways and more? I share it all! Join the exclusive Southern Sleuths private group today! Go to www.patreon.com/Tonyakappesbooks

As a special thank you for joining, you'll get an exclusive copy of my cross-over short story, *A CHARMING BLEND.* Go to Tonyakappes.com and click on subscribe at the top of the home page.

PREVIEW

As I rode, I couldn't help but think about last night's emergency council meeting again. The room had been packed with passionate citizens, and the tension had been palpable. I recalled the way Danielle, the environmentalist, stood up and argued against the proposed country-club development. She had discovered a natural spring on the land, and many of us agreed that it shouldn't be disturbed. She even had a gorgeous slideshow with photos.

I was relieved when the council voted down the project, but I knew some of our neighbors were still furious. The look on the developer's face was unforgettable. Especially when he looked at Leandar Taylor, the local real estate agent who'd sold him the land.

As I approached the contested land, I spotted the unmistakable flash of red-and-blue lights in the darkness near the lake.

My heart skipped a beat, and I slowed my bike, curiosity getting the better of me.

What could be happening at this hour? I wondered, my thoughts racing.

I pulled off the road and got off my bike. I walked cautiously toward the commotion, the gravel crunching under my feet. The sounds of the woods around me seemed to grow louder— the wind rustling through the trees and the distant hoot of an owl. My heart pounded in my chest as I drew closer to the scene.

“Stop right there!” I heard Sheriff Spencer Shepard call out with his gun drawn in front of him and pointing directly at me.

“It’s me. Roxy!” I yelled and sort of slumped down, just in case he fired.

"Roxy, what are you doing here?" Sheriff Spencer Shepard called out, his brow furrowed with concern.

"I was just on my way to open the Bean Hive when I saw the lights," I explained, my voice barely above a whisper. "What's going on, Spencer?"

The sheriff hesitated then spoke in a somber tone. "Someone was out for an early-morning jog and found a body."

A chill ran down my spine, and my stomach tightened.

A body? In our peaceful town?

I couldn't wrap my head around it. I glanced around, searching for answers, when the moon slipped out from behind a cloud. Its silvery light illuminated the scene like a spotlight, revealing the lifeless form of Leandar Taylor.

CHAPTER ONE

I knew the smell anywhere.

It wasn't the aroma of the freshly brewed coffee that filled the air at the Bean Hive, my coffee shop, and it wasn't the smell of the warm and inviting pastries filling the glass display counters. Nor was it the scent of the strong and rich aromas from the espresso coming from the hissing espresso machine.

"Good morning, Loretta." It was Loretta Bebe's perfume wafting through the coffee shop as soon as she walked in, adding an extra layer to the sensory experience.

She must have literally bathed in the stuff because as soon as she flung the door open, the stench of her perfume saturated every corner of the small coffee shop.

"I have no idea how you do it, Roxy." She had already made it to the counter before I'd turned around to actually put eyes on her. "You know it's me before you even look at me."

"You have a vibe." I smiled and watched her pluck the gloves off her hands, finger by finger, before she neatly laid them over the top of and between the handles of her pocketbook.

I would never hurt Loretta's feelings in a million years. She'd probably not care, but still. The community had welcomed me with open arms a few years ago when I decided to leave my job as a lawyer to fulfill my dreams of opening my very own coffee shop. Granted, I was getting a divorce, but all of that was behind me.

Until it wasn't, and my ex, Kirk, and his wife, Jessica, brought their new baby in here to grab their daily afternoon cold brews.

Yeah.

"A vibe?" she asked, nervously raking her fingernails across the edges of her short black hair. "I bet it's the Cherokee in me."

"Yep, I betcha that's it, Low-retta." The sarcasm was thick as it came out of Bunny Bowowski's mouth as she did a drive-by behind me with a couple of customer orders on her tray. Her soft gray hair was parted to the side and cut at chin length. She didn't bother wearing the shirt with the coffee shop's logo I'd purchased for the employees to wear.

Bunny and her best friend, Mae Belle Donovan, had started a knitting club that met at the coffee shop every Sunday afternoon during the winter. Instead of the Bean Hive shirt, Bunny always wore a shawl she knitted, clasping it with a fancy pin.

Honey Springs was a tourist town on Lake Honey Springs in Kentucky, and the tourists didn't really come during the snowy winters, which allowed me to have different operating hours for each season. It only made sense to close the shop on Sunday, making it a perfect spot for Bunny and her group. I wasn't sure what they'd do about the new spring hours when we opened for a few hours after church. I didn't ask. Bunny always had a plan.

"I wasn't talkin' to you, Bunny." Loretta snarled. The white line where the tanning bed couldn't reach showed when she crinkled her nose. "I don't know why you keep her around. She's not good for business."

"Bunny?" I asked Loretta. I turned my back on her so I could make her usual black coffee and disguise the smile on my face, knowing Bunny was getting Loretta's goat. "Everyone loves her." I pointed my chin into the coffee shop for Loretta to turn and look at the customer Bunny had in stitches about something she was saying.

"She's harmless." I put the coffee down next to the register and looked at my elderly employee.

Bunny Bowowski waddled over to the next table, and by the way the customer waved their hand in the air, I knew Bunny was asking them if she could get them anything else.

"You're a saint for putting up with her," Loretta said. The line of bracelets jingled and jangled as she fiddled with the zipper of her wallet to retrieve money.

I smiled. If you only knew that was what people say to me about you, I thought to myself.

"That's the girl from the environmental office," Loretta said about the customer in the corner. "I can't believe what they are thinking about doing down there past the Cocoon Inn."

"You said the key words." I took the money Loretta had tucked in between her fingers, admiring how her long red nails shone. I stuck the cash in the register. "'Thinking about.'" I straightened out the information card for the pet of the week Louise Carlton had left on the counter before I grabbed the carafe of freshly brewed coffee to go and fill up customers' cups.

It was free refills, and the fuller their mugs were, the more they ate, and that's where I made the most money.

Pet of the week was a feature I offered to the Pet Palace, the local SPCA, where I kept one of the animals in the coffee shop for the week to help out with their adoptions. There were many hoops we had to jump through with the local health department when I opened the Bean Hive, but it was well worth the hassle when an animal was adopted.

It was kinda like one of those cat cafés but with more than just cats. This week, Louise had brought in the cutest speckled puppy. I knew it wouldn't take long before someone adopted him.

Currently, he was snuggled up against Pepper, my gray schnauzer, who was a staple around here. Me and Patrick, my husband, also had a black standard poodle, Sassy. Sassy loved to go to Cane Constructions with Patrick. Really, I think she liked riding around to the various sites in his big truck with her head out the window.

"We have to talk!" The voice was loud enough to catch my attention and take me out of my conversation with Loretta. Not only did I look, but everyone must've also heard because the chatter inside the Bean Hive had ceased.

With the handle of the coffee carafe in my hand, I twisted around to see what all the ruckus was about.

It was Leandar Taylor, a local Realtor.

At five feet, ten inches, he had a lean and athletic build in his charcoal-gray tailored suit. The coat was open, and his crisp white dress shirt was tight enough to show he must work out with weights. He wore a leather belt, and when he pointed at Danielle, the cuff of his suit coat inched up enough to expose the designer watch on his wrist.

My mom had mentioned Leandar before and commented on his polished image.

I'd never met the man, and today wasn't a great example of a first meeting.

"I'm sorry, but I'm having my breakfast," Danielle said to him, but her eyes were shifting left to right to see if anyone was looking.

Now everyone *was* staring.

Danielle was a woman of striking appearance. She had chestnut-brown hair that tumbled down her back in loose waves. Her eyes were a piercing shade of emerald green and blinked back what I thought was a look of grave concern on her face.

"I don't care. We have to talk and talk now." He shoved his big finger in her face and tapped the toe of his fancy black snakeskin boots with toe brass. "You won't get away with these lies. I've already got a call in to your boss, and I know your history. When he calls me back, you bet I'm going to pull that card."

"Please leave me alone," she whispered. Red blotches started to crawl up her neck. "I'm more than happy to meet with you at the site or somewhere else later this evening."

She pulled out what appeared to be a day planner from the bag on the floor.

"I don't want no stinking appointment. Right here and right now."

Leandar's demands were enough for me to put the carafe down and go over to tell him to leave or tell them to take whatever was going on between them outside on the pier. I hurried around the counter and grabbed a hot drink Bunny had just made for a customer.

"I'll leave you alone and won't tell your boss about you if you do what is right." Leandar planted the palms of his hands flat against the table and got up in Danielle's face. "You only have yourself to blame for what is coming your way."

"Excuse me. Leandar, right?" I interrupted him and looked at the hot drink. I couldn't help but notice those fancy brass fittings on the toe of his boots had his initials engraved on them.

"Here's a delicious cappuccino for you." I read the label before I shoved it into his face. "Please enjoy it outside."

"I didn't order a cappuccino, and the name says 'Frank.'" He read off the name we'd written on it.

"It's on the house." I gestured for him to leave.

His lips curled in, and his nostrils flared like a bull's before it rushed a matador. His eyes bore into mine.

"I'd like you to leave my coffee shop now." I pinched out a smile. "And I'll be sure to tell my mama, Penny Bloom, you said hello."

Mentioning my mama was something I rarely did to scare off people. She wasn't at all scary, but I'd heard her talk about Leandar. He and my mama were in the same industry.

Real estate agents.

It was a competitive business, and there weren't very many in Honey Springs. But they had their own little network, and Leandar knew if word got around he was making a scene, it wouldn't go well with the others in their little circle.

So I used Mama to get his attention in this situation.

And I would be sure to tell her he stopped in.

His eyes moved past my shoulder, and he gave one more good, hard, and scary stare at Danielle. Poor lady, her hives had almost covered her entire neck area and were now creeping up to her jaw.

"I'll see you later." He held up Frank's cappuccino. "Thanks for the coffee. Tell Penny we need to get together soon."

"Oh, I'll tell her," I muttered behind my gritted-teeth smile. "To stay far away from you," I finished saying after he shut the door behind him. I turned around to face Danielle. "I'm so sorry. Are you okay?" I asked, pulling out the empty seat at the small café table to sit.

"I've lost my appetite." She pushed the plated strawberry scone away from her. "I'm sorry he made such a scene."

"It's okay. I'm sorry he did that to you." I pointed to her hands and forearms where more hives had popped up.

"I get hives when people confront me." She snorted and placed her hands in her lap. "Nothing a little prednisone can't fix." She pulled a bottle out of the workbag sitting on the floor.

"Wow." I laughed. "People confront you often?"

"In this line of business, they do." Danielle had been coming into the Bean Hive for a couple of weeks every morning.

She'd introduced herself but never told me why she was in town.

"So you're in Honey Springs for business?" I asked.

"Yes. Initially, I was hired by Blackwood Associates to come and evaluate a potential piece of property down past the local inn for a new country-club development," she confirmed. "But then there were some findings coming back that I'd sent off some samples of, and honestly, I'm hoping Blackwood Associates will rethink the location if they still want to use Honey Springs."

There were rumors of a big country club coming to Honey Springs, and I'd heard rumblings about it during one of our chamber of commerce meetings. Golf didn't interest me, so I didn't listen very closely to the debate, but when there was a country club being built, I would definitely try to get in front of the owners or shareholders to get my coffee in there.

After all, now that we had the space with the roastery next door, I was making all sorts of my own concoctions. I could easily make a blend just for a country club.

"What are you looking for when these companies hire you?" I asked, very curious now.

"It depends, but mainly things like environmental impacts of the proposed development. This assessment would involve studying the local ecosystem, habitats, and species, as well as understanding how construction and operation of the country club might affect the environment." From what it sounded like, she was saying Blackwood Associates really did care about the areas where they planned to build, which seemed rather nice.

"I think that's wonderful." I had to talk a little louder because the Bean Hive was filled with the morning customers chatting and enjoying their drinks. "I'm all about keeping Honey Springs a tourist destination where visitors come to enjoy the nature and beauty."

Honey Springs was a wonderful place not only for couples to come to stay in one of the cozy cabins the town had to offer for romantic getaways but also for families to enjoy Lake Honey Springs.

The Bean Hive was located on the boardwalk along with several other little locally owned mom-and-pop shops.

I glanced over at the counter. Bunny had restocked the variety of pastries, muffins, and biscuits, and my baristas were busy taking orders and making drinks. It wasn't until after the roastery was up and running that I'd had to hire two new full-time employees. I still kept the afternoon shift for the local high schoolers who worked for me.

The sounds of the espresso machines hissing and the spoons clinking against ceramic mugs were comforting to me, were enough for me to realize life had gone back to normal in the coffeehouse.

"I'm sure Leandar heard about some of my initial findings because he's standing to gain over half a million in commission from the sale of the land alone, not even including what they will give him for the condominiums they are going to build." As Danielle told me about the plans Blackwood Associates had made for the lakefront property, the more I wished I'd paid attention during the chamber meetings.

"You said something about findings that might make the community change their minds." She nodded, and I continued, "What do you do then?"

I didn't ask about what she found. If Bunny was here, she'd get the information, no problem. But I didn't want to seem too nosy yet.

"I'll be visiting the site to engage with local stakeholders, such as community members, local organizations, and government officials. They could be providing information about the potential environmental impacts, discussing mitigation measures, or soliciting feedback on the proposed development. Blackwood Associates are very involved with the communities where they build." She stood up and gathered her things.

Standing at five foot eight, Danielle appeared to be athletic, from what I would bet had been from years spent exploring the great outdoors.

Her sun-kissed skin bore the marks of a life spent in the elements, with a smattering of freckles across her nose and cheeks. Her style was practical and functional. She was often seen wearing cargo pants, sturdy boots, and lightweight jackets that allowed her to navigate the rugged terrain with ease.

"If you'll excuse me." She pushed in the chair, and I stood up. "I need to make some calls. I'm afraid my reports for your lake town have now turned to advocating for the protection of the lake and its surrounding environment around the development."

"Oh. That doesn't sound good," I blurted out.

"If you want to save Honey Springs, I suggest you come to the emergency meeting I'm going to ask your mayor to hold tonight." She shook her head, leaving me standing there feeling gut punched.

"I told you, she's up to somethin' 'round here." I hadn't heard Loretta walk up behind me. Her accent had taken a fifty-degree dive.

I knew that accent, and it was never followed up by anything good.

"Excuse me." A gentleman with glasses came up to me. "I'm Frank. Did you just give my cappuccino away?"

CHAPTER TWO

"Emergency meeting." Aunt Maxi vigorously rubbed her hands together. "I can't imagine what the mayor has to say that couldn't wait until next month's real meeting."

Aunt Maxi had come into the Bean Hive later that afternoon after word got around town about the emergency meeting.

"Danielle Quillen, the environmentalist hired by Blackwood Associates, has been coming in here every morning. She's been assessing the land where they want to develop the proposed country club," I said.

The afternoon staff were students from Honey Springs High School. I'd been blessed to be able to work with the economics teacher there and let them use the kitchen in the back of the coffee shop as well as teach them a few things about running a business. They'd even been able to open and run their own school coffee shop using the funds, and, of course, my deep discount on coffee, to help raise money for the home-economics department for updated supplies. It didn't just involve coffee supplies—I'm talking anything they needed for their projects.

Most of the students I'd met had really taken to the coffee side, and when they applied for the job, I had hired three of them. It freed up so much of my time.

It wasn't like they were actually roasting the beans or making the pastries. After a certain time in the afternoon, we only offered coffees and what was left in the display cases.

While Aunt Maxi and I waited for the emergency council meeting to start, she came into the kitchen with me and helped me clean up all the dirty dishes accumulated throughout the day and get some of tomorrow's pastries and food items out of the freezer so they could thaw overnight.

"She mentioned how she'd found something on the property or in the report that would pretty much change the fate of the club." I shrugged as I walked over to the walk-in freezer where I pulled out a tray of frozen quiches I'd made ahead of time.

"Oh dear." Aunt Maxi's brows knotted. The lines around her eyes were getting much deeper.

Aunt Maxi was inching up to seventy years old, and though it wasn't elderly, she was starting to slow down more and more each year. I loved her so much.

Honey Springs was never my physical home. Aunt Maxi, Maxine Bloom, was my home. When Kirk and I had gotten divorced, I didn't move to where Penny, my mom, lived. It was here in Honey Springs where I ran to seek comfort.

It was in Aunt Maxi's arms where I found the home I'd always needed. Honey Springs had always felt cozy to me. My father, before he died, brought me here every summer to visit Aunt Maxi. Sometimes he'd leave me here for weeks, months even. And that's how I met Patrick Cane.

He was my first-ever boyfriend, but because of a little misunderstanding between two lovesick teenagers, life happened, and I moved on. I went to college then eventually law school, where I met Kirk.

When my heart was broken, it was to Honey Springs I ran. Aunt Maxi just so happened to own a few buildings on the boardwalk, and the council had invested a lot of money to revitalize the touristy spot. Aunt Maxi had the grand idea I should take the empty building and make something of it.

It was a no-brainer to turn the building into a much-needed coffee shop, and it was already equipped with the kitchen due to the fact it had been a diner before. Here we stood today.

The Bean Hive, now a Honey Springs staple.

"She didn't tell you what it was?" Aunt Maxi eased down on one of the stools butted up to the workstation island in the middle of the large kitchen and helped herself to a piece of the coffee cake I'd just taken out of the oven.

She reached across the island and dragged the butter dish over to her, knifing a large chunk to smother the piece of coffee cake before she took a big bite out of it.

"She didn't. In fact, she said they would address it at the meeting. But you've not heard the best part." I looked at the clock because we had just enough time to have a cup of coffee. And like I loved to say around here, the gossip was just as hot as the coffee.

"Leandar Taylor came in here demanding to talk to her." My words made Aunt Maxi's brows go from a knot to a large arch.

"Do tell me all of it." Aunt Maxi held the coffee up in both hands and leaned on the island, her forearms holding her up.

That was one thing I loved about owning the Bean Hive. The connections.

There was just some sort of human connection that made us want to gather with others to talk and share stories in an innate way of bonding and fostering a sense of belonging as we sipped on coffee. Though no one wanted to claim we were gossiping, we totally were, but it created strong relationships and built trust among us.

I thought that was what the Bean Hive had become to the community over the years. Not only a place to come grab a hot cup of coffee but also an atmosphere that fostered a warm, cozy atmosphere that helped people relax and unwind.

The act of sitting around a table with friends and a hot beverage was comforting and calming, allowing people to escape from daily stresses and responsibilities.

Aunt Maxi sitting there right now did that for me. It was stressful for me to tell Leandar to leave. Like I mentioned, he was one of just a couple Realtors in the area, and he knew a lot of people.

"I'm not sure what he was yelling at her about. Danielle kept her cool and said that he'd find out about it at the emergency meeting." I took a sip of the coffee. "He was so mad. I told him to leave."

"You did?" Aunt Maxi shook her head. "When was this?"

"I don't know. I don't recall the time. It was this morning because Danielle was eating breakfast. She told him to let her eat her breakfast." I didn't know the exact wording, but it was enough to tell Aunt Maxi. "Something like that." I handed her a napkin.

"No wonder he was mad at the estate sale walk-through." Aunt Maxi's shoulders bounced when she laughed.

"Estate sale?" I wondered why she'd not invited me. I loved to use old pieces of china and mismatched items in the shop.

I glanced over at the cow creamers I'd gotten from Wild and Whimsy Antiques, a shop a few buildings down the boardwalk.

"Did they have any creamers?" They were so charming, just an added touch to the cute coffee shop when they were filled with cream and sitting on the table for the customer to doctor up their coffees the way they liked.

"It wasn't an actual sale." Aunt Maxi used the napkin to wipe the crumbs from her mouth that'd stuck to her bright-orange lipstick. "The Featherstones have the farm out on Gutter Road."

I'd never been there, but I knew it was a large piece of farmland.

"They've gotten so many offers from different horse-breeding farms up near Keeneland because the soil tested so good for limestone." Aunt Maxi knew all the ins and outs on the history of the property and their families.

Limestone was huge around here since we had the lake, but it also made for great vitamins and minerals for the racehorses. One of Kentucky's largest money-making industries was horse racing.

So to hear her say someone wanted the large farm for their horses didn't surprise me. There were many farms around here where people not only kept their racehorses but also trained them locally.

"I can't believe they are selling." I pushed back off the island and took her plate and our cups to clean since it was almost time for us to go to the meeting.

"I couldn't believe it either. I thought for sure Raffery Featherstone was going to keep that place forever. He's the sixth-generation owner, but that's what happens when your kids go off and leave home, not ever wanting to come back to the family business."

"I guess so." I gnawed on my lip, thinking about Raffery's kids. Who on earth wouldn't want a farm and estate like theirs to be handed down to them? Man. What a waste. I kept those thoughts to myself.

If I opened my mouth about leaving a legacy or mentioning children, Aunt Maxi would start harping on me and my biological clock.

For now, Patrick and I were good with our four-legged fur babies.

"Anyways." Aunt Maxi had gotten up and walked over to the coat-tree inside the kitchen's back door to get her big hobo bag. It landed with a thump when she put it on the island. "Leandar was there to try to get the sale. You know, be the Realtor. Penny was there too."

She dug down into her bag.

"What on earth were you doing there?" I asked, untying my apron and placing it on one of the free pegs on the coat-tree.

"I was thinking on making an offer to buy it without a Realtor, but the place is too darn nice to get a good deal. But when they do put it up for auction, you're gonna die when you get a look at the fine bone china." She knew I was a sucker for good dishes for the coffee shop.

"Don't tease me," I begged and pointed to her when I saw her take out her big can of hairspray. "Don't spray that in—" I let go of a long sigh.

I wasn't able to get out the words quick enough before she pressed her finger down on the nozzle with one hand and used her other hand to rack her short, this-season-blond-colored hair to high heaven to stay in place.

"Oopsy." She grimaced. "Just another little spray." With her finger pressed down on the nozzle of the can, she did one more sweep around her head, just for good measure, before she moved on to reapplying her lipstick.

"I guess Leandar didn't really care too much about what Danielle had done, or he would've still been mad at the Featherstones." I grabbed Pepper's leash off the coatrack and motioned for Aunt Maxi to follow me out the swinging kitchen door into the coffee shop.

The health department made it very clear about no animals being allowed into the kitchen. It was one rule I did live by because I didn't want to be shut down.

I gave the coffee shop a good once-over to make sure there wasn't anything left undone for me to do to get ready for a smooth morning tomorrow. I liked to have as many things completed and ready as possible, so when I did open early in the morning at four thirty, I had little or nothing to do.

With the afternoon employees already working on the closing checklist and the puppy from the Pet Palace well taken care of, Aunt Maxi and I were off to see exactly why the mayor had called this emergency meeting.

The meetings were always at the event center on the boardwalk, All About the Details. It was due to the fact the courthouse was located in downtown Honey Springs, and though it was literally about a ten-minute walk—three minutes on a bicycle, the most preferred mode of transportation—a lot of citizens came to the meetings. There weren't any rooms in the old courthouse to hold that many people.

By law, the meetings had to be open to the public, and it just made sense to have them at the big event center on the boardwalk.

"Save me a seat," I told Aunt Maxi as I prepared to take Pepper to the grass off the far end of the boardwalk to let him do his business so I could sit through the entire meeting without him interrupting to go potty.

She disappeared inside All About the Details while Pepper and I hightailed it past Buzz-In-And-Out Diner, Honey Comb Salon, and Wild and Whimsy Antiques, stopping briefly when something in the antique's store display window caught my eye.

Pepper pulled, extending his leash to full capacity, not allowing me time to get a good look at the cute antique cake stands that would look good sitting on top of the glass display cases in the coffee shop.

I made a mental note to ask Dan or Beverly Teagarden, the owners, about the cake stands.

Pepper practically dragged me down the boardwalk steps where the grassy area and the beach area of Lake Honey Springs met. He ventured along the grass toward the water's edge, and before I knew it, we were at the water.

I stood at the edge of Lake Honey Springs, feeling the soft grass beneath my sneakers as Pepper sniffed around for the perfect spot to do his business. My gaze shifted to the marina on my left, a picturesque scene filled with boats bobbing gently in the sparkling water.

To my right, the gorgeous Cocoon Inn stood proudly, its exterior welcoming visitors from near and far. The double-decker porches with the rocking chairs looked all occupied.

I sighed, taking in the idyllic scene that was about to be disrupted by the chaos of the emergency council meeting. My thoughts kept going back to the meeting. There was something not settling right in my bones, and that was never a good thing.

The boardwalk buzzed with activity, people meandering in and out of the quaint, cozy shops that lined the waterfront. Laughter and conversation filled the air, mingling with the distant sound of seagulls crying overhead. I tried to appreciate the moment, but my thoughts were consumed by the meeting and the mysterious findings in Danielle's report.

Danielle's cryptic words hung over me like a dark cloud.

"The community will change its mind about letting the company build."

But she hadn't given me any more information, leaving me to anxiously await the emergency meeting called by the mayor.

A cool spring breeze rustled through the leaves overhead, and it made me wish I'd brought the jacket from the Bean Hive with me. The sun was deceiving on these spring days. During the day, it was warm and almost hot, but in the evenings, as it was setting, the breeze off the lake made it so much cooler.

The scent of blossoming flowers filled my nostrils, and I closed my eyes for a moment, trying to calm my racing thoughts. The sounds of Lake Honey Springs—the gentle lapping of water against the shore, the rustling of leaves, and the chirping of birds—usually brought me comfort. But today, they only added to my unease.

Pepper, seemingly oblivious to my inner turmoil, bounded back to me, his tail wagging energetically. I reached down to pat his head, his soft fur offering a brief moment of solace amidst my concerns. He looked up at me with his big brown eyes, as if to say, "Everything will be okay." I took a deep breath, trying to hold on to that comforting thought.

"Roxy!" I heard someone call behind me and away from the lake. "Roxanne!"

I turned around to see Camey Montgomery, the owner of the Cocoon Inn, standing still on the concrete sidewalk that ran between the inn and the boardwalk.

"Are you going to the meeting?" she hollered to me as Pepper and I walked closer.

"I am. Are you?" I called out to her, but by the time she responded, we were already standing next to her and she was bent down, patting Pepper.

"Yes. We can walk together." She stood up and greeted me with a hug. "It has to be about the development."

"I know it is." I nodded to confirm. We walked side by side, only stopping briefly when Pepper would catch a scent. "The environmentalist Blackwood Associates hired has been coming into the coffee shop. She mentioned today the mayor had read her findings and she asked him to call this emergency meeting."

I didn't bother telling her about Leandar Taylor because telling her would be gossiping, and there was no need for that since once Danielle was done with her job, she'd be leaving Honey Springs and we'd probably never see her again.

"Do you know something?" I asked Camey, curious to why she'd mentioned it the way she did.

"There's been people there all day long. I can see it from the honeymoon-suite balcony." Camey ran the inn like a five-star hotel. Though she had employees, Camey had her hand in all the areas and little details that made the inn so homey to all her guests. "I was sweeping up there, getting it ready for a newlywed couple coming in this weekend for the start of their honeymoon, when I saw people standing way past the lake and in the weeds of the area. I wasn't sure what they were looking at, but Quentin told me his cousin worked in the public works, and they were called there to look at something."

"Public-works employee? Really?" I questioned, wondering what on earth they had to do with the land.

"It's state property, and if they found anything on there that would need to be preserved, there's no way the state will let them build." Camey should know.

The historic white mansion, built in 1841, had been in Camey's family for years. Camey had hired Cane Construction to help rebuild the old structure into an amazing hotel that was situated right on Lake Honey Springs and kept its cozy character. The two-story white brick building with porches across both stories was something to behold, especially when you were standing on the beachfront in front of the property, looking back.

Gorgeous.

"I guess we'll find out soon." I nodded toward the door going into All About the Details when the mayor shuffled in ahead of us.

I took one more look out at Lake Honey Springs. Sunset was one of my favorite times of day. It was beginning to set, casting golden rays across the water and bathing the bustling boardwalk in a warm glow. As the shadows grew longer, so did my sense of foreboding.

What could be so important that the mayor would call an emergency meeting? The future of our beloved Lake Honey Springs hung in the balance, and all I could do was wait, hope, and prepare for the storm that was coming.

CHAPTER THREE

Alice Dee Spicer wildly waved her arms in the air as soon as she caught my eye from the back of the filled room. I'd not seen the room this filled since Patrick and I had come to the chamber of commerce Christmas party.

Alice was the president of the Beautification Committee, which made her an automatic member of the town council. She was sitting in front with all the other town officials, facing the crowd from behind a large banquet table.

She pointed, gesturing at a place for Camey and me to sit.

"Up here." I nudged Camey. She was looking around for a spot before I gestured to Helen.

"Lordy." Camey nervously patted around her scarlet hair before raking her fingers down her thick bangs. "Alice just wants us to sit there so she can stare at my hair."

"Your hair?" I snorted and picked up Pepper so I didn't have to worry about him sniffing everyone's shoes when we passed. "Your hair looks great."

Alice was the owner of Honey Comb, the local beauty salon.

"Alice doesn't think so. I canceled my hair appointment the other afternoon because Amelia had a spring play at school. It was during the middle of the day, the day before their spring break started." Camey spoke out of the side of her mouth as we maneuvered our way down the right side of the aisle around the crowd. "She told me how my bangs needed to be cut and thinned out and refused to cancel my appointment."

"Refused?" I glanced around my shoulder to look at her but kept walking up the aisle.

"Yes. She hung up on me." She snorted and rolled her eyes. "Hi, Helen."

Camey gave Alice a little wave before we noticed there was only one seat. Apparently, Alice had only gestured for me.

"You take it." I waved a hand. "I will sit on the floor with Pepper."

"No," Camey insisted. "She obviously meant it for you." Camey glared at Alice, but she had already turned to talk to someone else.

"Here." Big Bib was sitting in the row behind us and offered Camey his seat. He was sitting next to Aunt Maxi, who was already situated in the chair with her big hobo bag nestled in her lap. Her hands were clasped on top. "I might have to leave soon, so you take it."

"No." Camey shook her head.

"Then someone else will." The big, burly, but softhearted boat mechanic and owner of the marina was dressed in his usual overalls that looked like he'd just poured an entire container of oil down them.

"Thank you," Camey said.

"I tried to save you a seat." Aunt Maxi had eased up on the edge of her seat and whispered. "What took you so long?"

"Pepper." I ran my hand down my sweet pup, who was more than happy to be sitting on my lap. "He had to do his business."

"Sweet baby." Aunt Maxi reached around me and patted his head. "Why is Penny up there?"

She pointed out how Mom and Leandar Taylor sat on the stage, as well as Danielle Quillen and another gentleman and woman I didn't know.

As I scanned the room, my eyes landed on a man I didn't recognize. He was tall, standing at around six-one, with a lean, athletic build that demanded attention. His wavy, jet-black hair fell just below his ears, accentuating his chiseled jawline and partially hiding his deep blue eyes.

His slight tanned skin hinted at his love for outdoor adventures, and I couldn't help but notice the faint lines around his eyes, suggesting that he was no stranger to laughter and smiling.

He had a day or two's worth of stubble, which only added to his rugged charm.

He was dressed in a casual style that suited him. He wore a tailored shirt with the sleeves rolled up, revealing his toned forearms, and paired it with well-fitting jeans. His leather boots completed the ensemble, giving him an air of effortless sophistication.

I found it impossible not to be drawn to the man's charismatic presence and could tell the others near him felt the same.

"If I could all have your attention, we'd like to start the meeting," the mayor said through the microphone at the podium, silencing the room. "As you know, Blackwood Associates has been in town over the past six to nine months, give or take. They have been interested in building a new community that includes a country club, a swim club, and a neighborhood surrounding it, past Cocoon Inn."

The mayor pointed out to a plan on a hardboard propped up on a tripod. It looked like a blue print of a plot of land.

There was a bit of shuffling coming from Leandar Taylor. That was enough movement to have caught my eye.

"Blackwood Associates has hired Danielle Quillen, a well-known environmentalist, to survey the land, take samples, and make sure the land is environmentally sound or viable for such a project." The mayor really didn't seem like he understood all the words, so he passed it off to Danielle. "She can best explain it."

Danielle got up from her seat and smiled as she passed the mayor on her way up to the podium.

"Thank you," she said into the microphone and nodded over her shoulder to the mayor. "Like the mayor said, this is Caspian Blackwood," she said.

While everyone gave notice to Caspian, I watched Danielle set down and flip open the folder I'd seen many times on top of her table at the Bean Hive.

"When I took the job and came to Honey Springs, I found a delightful group of citizens that.were welcoming and who love their town. In fact, no one was unhappy that a large developer wanted to come in and take up all this lakefront. They simply told me they wanted to make sure the land around the development wouldn't be compromised."

She took a moment to pause, and if I could read her body language, I felt like she was trying to compose what she was going to say and make sure it came out properly.

"With the help of local Realtor, Leandar Taylor—" As soon as she said his name, Caspian groaned, rolled his neck, and looked opposite of Leandar, making it seem as though the mere mention of Leandar's name made him ill. Danielle continued, "He was able to provide us with a plot and helped get the property in question staked off."

She had a clicker in her hand that I'd noticed, and when she pushed it, a slide of photos popped up on the screen offstage.

There were photos of the entire process she'd done to get an accurate report.

There was a shot taken from the lake's edge of the sun sinking low in the sky. The glass-like surface of the water contrasted with the trees in the background from the small island in the middle of Lake Honey Springs.

"It was beautiful to stand there and look at this wonderful piece of land your entire town has preserved over the years." She lifted up items as she talked about them. "Armed with my notebook, my camera, and a collection of scientific equipment, I began my investigation."

As she talked, the buzz of the clicker as she pushed the button was the only sound in the entire building. The slides went along with her story.

It was a story that captured everyone's attention.

Even Pepper's.

She went on to tell us how she'd meticulously examined the soil, tested the water quality, and identified the local flora and fauna. As she wandered through the site, she said she couldn't shake the feeling that there was something unique about this place, something she couldn't quite put her finger on.

"As I ventured deeper into the forest surrounding the lake, the air grew cooler, and the once lively sounds of the woodland creatures began to quiet. I stumbled upon a small hidden clearing carpeted in lush green moss and surrounded by tall ancient trees. At the center of the clearing, a crystal-clear spring bubbled up from the earth, its waters shimmering in the fading light." When she showed the photos she'd taken, the entire audience gasped.

She looked out into the crowd, and it showed on her face that she was taken aback because none of us knew that was there.

"I can see you are as shocked to see this as I was. I felt an overwhelming sense of awe when I realized that this spring was the source of the lake's pristine water." The significance of her discovery was not lost on her; she knew that the construction of a country club could threaten the delicate balance of this rare ecosystem.

"I have worked tirelessly with Leandar and Blackwood Associates, along with their investors, to convince them to rethink their plans and use their money for the good of Honey Springs to transform this area into a nature preserve." Danielle turned and pointed to Alice Dee Spicer. "I've included Alice Dee Spicer into the talks since she is the president of your Beautification Committee."

"I think we need to have a second opinion." Leandar stood up and protested.

"Sit down," Raffery Featherstone hollered out from the back. "Haven't you ruined enough of this already?"

That got everyone's attention.

"What did he ruin?" I overheard Aunt Maxi ask Camey. "Is that what he said?"

"If I could just say something." The voice drew us all back to look at the stage where Caspian had gotten up from his seat and walked over to the microphone. "This is why we hired Danielle."

Caspian was not without charm. He had a disarming smile that seemed to melt away any resistance he encountered, and he had a charisma that I could tell allowed him to secure deals that others would have thought impossible.

Even though he appeared to be a skilled negotiator, able to use his charm and wit to persuade even the most skeptical partners to see the potential in his projects, I wasn't buying his act.

Like I said, I've seen his kind before.

"I, too, find myself at odds with Danielle Quillen. Yes, we clashed over the fate of the land, but eventually she saw that I had to confront the consequences of these actions and reevaluate the priorities for why we wanted to bring this amazing country club to Honey Springs. The people." He drew his arms out in front of him. "We want to bring more and more people to Honey Springs to create even more of a small tourist town. It will bring so many new jobs to you, and that's growth. Leandar Taylor was the Realtor we had believed had full knowledge of the spring. We didn't know it was there."

Caspian was starting to create a case for him and his company. Another tactic I'd seen done in a court of law when cases such as these had already begun to build and there was no one there to stop them until someone with even the slightest bit of environmental knowledge found out it was hurting the earth.

"That's why we are going to continue looking for property in the area with the help of Penny Bloom." Caspian was about to lay out their plan.

"Save our land! Save our land!" Camey stood up, punching her fisted hand in the air to start the chant. "Save our land!"

It only took three chants for her to start the entire room yelling it and pointing to Caspian. The loudest in the room was Raffery Featherstone. He was louder than anyone in the room, probably because he was walking up the center aisle, his eyes focused on Leandar Taylor and pointing at Caspian Blackwood.

Raffery reached the tripod with the building plans on it and ripped them in half, throwing them up in the air.

The entire room erupted.

Even Pepper barked, but I knew it was my cue to get out of there.

There was nothing good going to come of what the emergency meeting was about. The only thing I felt was sadness for Patrick. He'd hoped Cane Construction was going to be able to bid on the job.

He'd had big plans for that money.

CHAPTER FOUR

The next morning, I sat on the front porch of the little cabin where Patrick and I lived, sipping a hot cup of steaming coffee and waiting for Sassy and Pepper to go potty before I needed to go to work.

They seemed to have found a new scent. The two of them stepped over each other to get a better sniff. I reached into the basket next to the rocking chair and took out a thin blanket to put over my lap as I waited. Thoughts of yesterday's emergency meeting had rolled around in my head all night, leaving me with little to no sleep.

I'd even turned on my book light at around one in the morning to read a few chapters of the cozy mystery I was reading, due to the fact I wanted to quiet my brain. When that didn't work, I just laid there, trying to think of something other than the piece of property with the spring that was literally between our cabin and the boardwalk.

Patrick and I had taken the dogs across the street and down to the lake so many times over the past few years. I found it odd we'd not stumbled upon it.

"Sassy." I sighed when I noticed her silhouette in the light from the moon, rolling around in something. "Your daddy isn't going to be happy about that."

I could hear Patrick now, fussing about having to give her a bath because she's stinking up our little home to high heaven.

When I first moved to Honey Springs, I knew the little cabin was exactly what I needed. It was small and inviting—even though it needed a lot of work—but charming and cozy. A great place to heal my heart and soul.

With the old knob-and-tube wiring long gone, I'd turned the cabin into a wonderful home. It was small. There was one big room with a combination kitchen and dining room.

The bathroom and laundry room were located on the far-back right. There was a set of stairs that led up to one big room that was considered the bedroom.

The natural light from the skylights and the large window in the bedroom really made the room inviting. After I'd added the white iron bed suite from Aunt Maxi's storage unit and a few quilts she'd had stored, the bedroom was cozy and perfect for us.

As much as I wanted to stay and snuggle in that morning, I had to get going or the coffee wouldn't be ready for opening at six thirty a.m.

It wasn't like I was going to have too much to do. As soon as I got the dogs inside, I went back to the laundry room where I kept my standard uniform work clothes, slipped something on, and prepared for the short five-minute bike ride to the boardwalk.

I had also prepared myself for all the gossip that would be flying around the Bean Hive. There was nothing like a good council meeting, death, wedding, or baby being born that brought the locals in to see what everyone else knew.

That was why I had taken a few more quiches, donuts, and various other pastries from the freezer before I left the coffee shop to go to the meeting.

Sassy wandered back up the steps to get back in bed with Patrick. It would be a few more hours before they'd get up and go to the office. Pepper stayed downstairs with me, looking at me with his big eyes as if he were telling me he was ready to go to work.

"Not today," I told him. His small tail fell. "It's going to be really busy, and it wouldn't be fair for you to have to listen to all that gossip. I don't even want to hear it. I love you too much to put that on you."

He followed me out of the laundry room and into the small kitchen, where I took a scoop of his food from one of the bottom cabinets in the small galley-style kitchen and poured it into his bowl.

Sadly, he walked into the family room where he laid down in his little bed in front of the potbelly stove. He loved to lie there during the winter months when it was roaring with a fire inside.

He rested his chin on the edge of his bed, looking at me with little hope that I'd agree to take him. He knew when I fed him there, he wasn't going to the shop.

"I love you, Pepper. You be a good boy." I plucked the keys from the hook next to the door, and I grabbed my bag from the coatrack.

A car wasn't necessary to get around town. I had a small car, but mainly it stayed parked during the warmer seasons, and I biked everywhere unless Patrick and I were going somewhere together.

There was a small wire basket attached to the front of the bike where Pepper fit perfectly when he came to work. Today, I threw my bag in there, flipped on the flashing light on the front, and headed out into the dark early morning.

The cool morning air bit at my cheeks as I pedaled along the familiar path to the Bean Hive coffee shop. The quiet hum of the bicycle chain and the rhythmic crunch of my tires on the gravel road formed a soothing soundtrack to my predawn ride. It was four thirty, and the world was still slumbering. My small lake town felt like a dream, with the dark woods on one side of the road and the peaceful lake on the other.

As I rode, I couldn't help but think about last night's emergency council meeting again. The room had been packed with passionate citizens, and the tension had been palpable. I recalled the way Danielle, the environmentalist, stood up and argued against the proposed country-club development. She had discovered a natural spring on the land, and many of us agreed that it shouldn't be disturbed. She even had a gorgeous slideshow with photos.

I was relieved when the council had voted down the project, but I knew that some of our neighbors were still furious. The look on the developer's face was unforgettable. Especially when he looked at Leandar Taylor, the local real estate agent who'd sold them the land.

As I approached the contested land, I spotted the unmistakable flash of red-and-blue lights in the darkness near the lake.

My heart skipped a beat, and I slowed my bike, curiosity getting the better of me.

"What could be happening at this hour?" I wondered, my thoughts racing.

I pulled off the road and got off my bike. I walked cautiously toward the commotion, the gravel crunching under my feet. The sounds of the woods around me seemed to grow louder—the wind rustling through the trees and the distant hoot of an owl. My heart pounded in my chest as I drew closer to the scene.

"Stop right there!" I heard Sheriff Spencer Shepard call out with his gun drawn in front of him and pointing directly at me.

"It's me. Roxy!" I yelled and sort of slumped down, just in case he fired.

"Roxy, what are you doing here?" Sheriff Spencer Shephard called out, his brow furrowed with concern.

"I was just on my way to open the Bean Hive when I saw the lights," I explained, my voice barely above a whisper. "What's going on, Spencer?"

The sheriff hesitated, then spoke in a somber tone. "Someone was out for an early-morning jog and found a body."

A chill ran down my spine, and my stomach tightened when the moon slipped out from behind a cloud, its silvery light illuminated the scene like a spotlight, revealing the lifeless form of Leandar Taylor.

My breath caught in my throat, and my eyes widened in shock. I knew Leandar but never imagined I'd see him like this. My emotions were a tangled mess of confusion, sadness, and fear.

Sheriff Spencer noticed my distress and placed a reassuring hand on my shoulder.

"I know this is tough, Roxy. But I'll need your help. If you saw or heard anything unusual, it might be important."

I nodded, swallowing hard. "Of course, Spencer. I'll do whatever I can. But are you saying this is foul play?"

Kevin Roberts, the local coroner, was already on the scene. I couldn't tell what he was doing because Spencer had held me back a little, plus it was still dark. The sun wouldn't come up for another couple of hours.

"If you want to call blunt-force trauma to the head 'homicide,' then yes." Spencer nodded.

As I stared at Leandar's body, the reality of the situation began to sink in.

Our cozy town had just become the setting for a chilling mystery, and I knew I couldn't rest until I helped uncover the truth.

CHAPTER FIVE

"It wasn't like he was telling me to go out and find clues." I told Bunny about what happened on my way into work and how Spencer had told me to keep my eyes and ears open. "He knows once news breaks this morning about Leandar, everyone will be talking."

"Why on earth would he need you?" Bunny shook her head and waddled around the coffee shop with the tray of cow coffee creamers. She was placing one on each café table and making sure all the little table condiment containers were filled so they were ready for when we flipped the sign on the door to Open.

I went down the line of the industrial coffee makers and flipped them on before I made my way over to the coffee bar, where we kept an honors system for customers who didn't want to wait in line to buy a simple black, hot coffee. The six thermoses I kept at all times at the coffee bar were ready to be put in place. I grabbed three and headed toward the end of the counter.

On my way over to the bar, I looked out the front windows. Since the Bean Hive was located in the middle of the boardwalk, right across from the pier, we had a gorgeous view of the lake.

The lake was holding a dark secret that only it knew, for now.

I shook the thought out of my head and placed the three industrial thermoses with different blends of my specialty coffees on the bar, one filled with a decaffeinated blend even though I never understood the concept of that.

But Aunt Maxi made sure I understood some people only drank the unleaded stuff. The coffee bar had everything you needed to take a coffee with you. Quickly, I walked back behind the counter to grab the other three.

Just as I placed them, my heart stopped and I jumped at the sound of the hard knock coming from someone at the front window.

"Let me in!" Aunt Maxi knocked again but harder.

"I oughta have known she'd be here this early. I'm gonna have to take me an aspirin." Bunny acted as though the sight of Aunt Maxi had given her a sudden headache.

On my way over to the door, I had a habit of glancing around to see if the coffee shop needed any repairs. It was something I'd done daily since I had redone the entire inside by myself after watching DIY YouTube videos.

The white shiplap I'd put on the walls could probably stand a fresh coat of paint, but currently there were bigger things to worry about.

Leandar Taylor.

And I was one hundred percent positive it was why Aunt Maxi was here this early.

Bunny had started to pull down the chalkboard menus that hung from the ceiling over the L-shaped glass countertop so she could write the daily specials on them.

"The first menu is the same," I called as I unlocked the door for Aunt Maxi. "All the pies and cookies are the same. And the tortes and quiches are too," I told her and decided to flip the sign because I knew people would be getting here much earlier this morning.

Sadly, it was how it worked.

"What needs to be changed?" Bunny glanced at the third chalkboard listing the lunch options, including soups and catering information.

“We have broccoli-cheddar soup today.” I sighed and gave Aunt Maxi a hug. “Did you hear?”

“Did I hear?” She jerked back. “The whole town has heard. You know, Gloria has already enacted the church’s telephone chain.”

Gloria Dei would know. She worked at the sheriff’s department.

“Leave it to y’all to gossip,” Bunny couldn’t resist the jab. “Poor man is dead, and you’re runnin’ y’all’s mouth about it.”

“Bunny, I don’t know who you think you are. Mae Belle Donovan already sold you out. She said you called her as soon as the telephone chain reached you. And she wasn’t even who you were supposed to call.” Aunt Maxi and Bunny Bowowski had what some would call a love-hate relationship friendship, but I knew I could wrangle them in on helping me get some ideas on who I needed to be listening for, since Spencer had asked me to do so.

“Okay, you two, we aren’t going to help Spencer out this way.” I caught Aunt Maxi’s ear on my way over to the tea bar on the opposite side of the counter from the coffee bar, which was where Aunt Maxi had gone to make herself a cup of coffee.

The tea bar had a nice selection of gourmet teas and loose-leaf teas along with cold teas. I’d even gotten a few antique teapots from Wild and Whimsy Antiques, which happened to be the first shop on the boardwalk. If a customer came in and wanted a pot of hot tea, I could fix it for them, or they could fix their own to their taste.

“You mean to tell me Spencer wants to endanger my only niece?” Aunt Maxi’s drawn-on brows rose.

“I love you, but it doesn’t take snooping around to know it was Caspian Blackwood.” Bunny had no problem saying out loud what I was thinking.

The distinct aroma of freshly brewed coffee, mixed with the scent of warm pastries, filled the air, wafting through the cozy space as I busied myself with the morning preparations.

As Bunny meticulously placed the pastries in the glass display case, her eyes twinkled with curiosity.

"You know, Roxy," Bunny began, "I've been thinking about Leandar's murder, and I can't help but suspect that Caspian Blackwood is involved. He's always been a shady character, and with the development being halted, he certainly had a motive."

This was one of those situations where I'd let the two of them mull over what each one of them had in their heads before I would mix their two ideas together and come up with a plan.

The three of us weren't exactly new to being nosy. We'd put ourselves in a couple of crime investigations over the years and, well, let's just say we've been able to come up with a good system on how to get things out of people. Spencer knew it, too, and that's why he'd asked me to keep my ear to the ground.

The soft clinking of cups and saucers could be heard as I arranged them on the counter.

Aunt Maxi nodded in agreement, her silver bracelets jingling as she arranged the tea selection. "As much as it pains me, I have to agree with Bunny. Caspian has the most to gain from Leandar's death, especially if it means the development can move forward. Just think of all that money Blackwood Associates has put into this development, and if Leandar would've just done his job before all this got started, he'd probably still be alive."

I mulled over their words, the gears in my mind turning. I hurried through the swinging door between the kitchen and the coffee shop to grab one of the whiteboards I used to write the specials on when I was in the kitchen.

"You both make a good point," I conceded as I headed back through the door.

I reached for a towel and wipe-off board. "We need to create a murder board to organize our thoughts and explore all possible suspects."

As I began to jot down names and motives, the scent of rich coffee beans enveloped us, providing a sense of comfort despite the grim task at hand. Problem was, I only had one suspect: Caspian Blackwood.

Aunt Maxi piped up, "We can't rule out Danielle Quillen, the environmentalist, either. She may have had good intentions in stopping the development, but who knows what lengths she would go to in order to protect that natural spring?"

Bunny chimed in, "And what about the potential investors of the development? We don't know who they are, but they must have had a vested interest in the project. They could have easily turned on Leandar if they felt their investment was at risk."

I nodded, adding their names and suggestions to the murder board. "We can't jump to conclusions. We need to keep an open mind and consider all possibilities."

As we continued discussing the case, the first customers of the day began to trickle into the Bean Hive. The lively chatter of our fellow townspeople filled the air, blending with the enticing aroma of coffee and freshly baked goods. We knew we had a long day ahead of us, but the prospect of solving Leandar's murder and restoring peace to our cozy town fueled our determination.

There was one person I knew I needed to see first. The person who was generally first in line as soon as I opened every morning but who wasn't here today.

Danielle Quillen.

"Do you know where Danielle is staying?" I asked Bunny a few hours later when the breakfast rush died down.

Aunt Maxi had left the shop to do whatever it was Aunt Maxi did during the day.

Bunny always held conversation with Danielle every morning since Danielle had been in town.

"I don't know. I'm guessing she's been paid by Blackwood Associates." Bunny pointed to the last quiche. "Can I take that with me to Floyd?"

"Of course. Take whatever you want." I didn't mind, and my thoughts were preoccupied with how I was going to get information on where to find Danielle.

I'd spent the morning watching the door at the coffee shop as customers entered, waiting for Danielle to come in like she'd done every single day for the last few weeks. Not today.

Suspicious?

I was.

You won't get away with these lies. I've already got a call into your boss, and I know your history. Leander's words were unsettling to me as I recalled them.

What lies?

If anyone besides Blackwood Associates had motive, it would be Danielle. Especially if the victim was about to uncover lies that were bad enough for her to lose her job.

"Then I'm off," Bunny said, taking me out of my thoughts. "Are you sure you don't mind if I go early?"

The bell over the door dinged, and in walked Crissy Lane. You couldn't miss that sun-washed blond hair from a mile away.

"I guess you don't mind." Bunny waved and stopped briefly to chat with Crissy.

Even if I did mind, Bunny wasn't going to stay. She'd already gotten her shawl all buttoned, her pocketbook in the crook of her arm, and her pillbox hat bobby-pinned in her hair.

"Go. Tell Floyd I said happy anniversary," I hollered to her after she and Crissy said goodbye.

"You remembered." Bunny had been telling me nonstop since the beginning of the year how this was her and Floyd's two-year dating anniversary.

They were cute. She cooked for him, and he was good companionship for her. Though she vowed she'd never get married again, I still had my doubts.

"Of course I remembered. Enjoy your date." I gestured for her to get on out of there and waved her off.

"I'll have me the usual." Crissy Lane's Southern accent was truly charming. Her long fake lashes batted above her freckled cheeks. "But give me an extra shot of espresso. I'm so tired. I got a call last night about raccoons in the dumpsters at the spa."

"Be Happy Spa is on an island." My brows knotted. "How did the raccoons get over there?"

"I reckon they swam over." She shook her head. "Now I've got to go over there and pick up trash. So the extra shot of caffeine will do me some good."

I had about one hour until the afternoon staff would get there. It was that weird transition time during the day when the coffee shop was at its slowest time.

There was only one customer, sitting at the bar along the front window and facing Lake Honey Springs as she worked on her computer. It was a great time to clean all the tables and make sure the condiments were filled and the coffee was fresh for the afternoon customers that were mainly schoolchildren who liked to come in after school and visit with their friends before they went home at night.

Then the coffee shop turned over in customers and became the after-dinner coffee drinkers who had supper along the boardwalk and stopped by for an after-dinner coffee while they sat on the boardwalk to stare out over Lake Honey Springs.

I should've been doing all the cleaning, but the one true chore that had to be done was the coffee. My mind wasn't into cleaning and refilling. The puppy was asleep in the puppy bed and the one customer was occupied, so I took a moment to run back to the kitchen and grab a bag of the coffee beans I'd roasted a week ago and the whiteboard that Aunt Maxi, Bunny, and I had written on earlier that morning.

There wasn't any news, only rumblings this morning in the coffee shop when practically the entire town had come in to gossip, but as the day went on, I was sure there'd be some sort of gossip, secrets let out.

I was banking on getting whatever secret Leandar had on Danielle to come out of hiding, but there was nothing. Or at least I'd not heard anything.

The customer was gone when I pushed back through the kitchen door, but I wasn't alone.

Loretta Bebe was standing at the counter, drumming her long hot-pink fingernails on top of the glass display.

"I was beginning to wonder if someone was here," she said in her slow Southern drawl, eyeballing me. "I guess I was right about the country club."

Loretta beamed with joy.

"I'm guessing that Raffery Featherstone did Leandar Taylor in." She looked at the whiteboard. "What is that?"

"It's nothing." I laid it facing down on the counter. "What is it you were saying about Raffery?"

"Don't tell me you've not thought about who killed Leandar, Roxy." Loretta batted her fake lashes at me. I swear, if she blinked them faster, she'd create a tornado, those things were so long and thick. "Raffery was selling his farm so he could use the money to invest in the golf course."

A smile crossed her lips.

"My, my." She laid her hand on her chest. Every single finger had some sort of ring with a large stone on it. "I know something you don't? I was guessing Penny had already filled you in on the whole situation."

"She has not, but you are right about one thing." This was one of those times when I knew Loretta Bebe just might be the gossip I'd been waiting for. "Why don't I heat you up the last piece of butter-pecan bread I made this morning to go with the freshly brewed cup of coffee I just made before you walked in, and we can compare notes."

I had to phrase it in such a way that Loretta would feel like she was getting something out of this too.

"I'll be right over there." She twisted around and pointed to the couch that sat in front of the coffee shop's fireplace, though it wasn't turned on. "We might be visiting for a minute, and I want to be comfortable."

"I'll be right there." I knew partnering with Loretta was going to cost me dearly if Aunt Maxi found out.

Aunt Maxi and Loretta were always at odds. Aunt Maxi had little to no tolerance for liars. According to Aunt Maxi, Loretta Bebe's tall tales about being part Cherokee tore Aunt Maxi up when we all know Loretta would sneak over to Lisa Stalh's garage for a good ol' fake-n-bake in that tanning bed.

To each their own, and right now, I needed to know what Loretta knew about Raffery Featherstone.

After starting all the industrial coffeepots brewing for the arrival of the afternoon customers and plating Loretta's piece of bread with a pat of butter, just like she liked it, I headed over to the couch.

"Here you go." I set the small tray on the coffee table in front of her, along with the cow creamer. She always commented on how cute it was with the little cowbell dangling around its neck, filled with the Italian sweet cream she liked. "Italian sweet cream."

"Low-fat, I hope." She rubbed her belly and winked.

"Yes, that," I lied, but she knew it as I winked back. "I also wanted to show you this," I told her as my voice carried to her while I grabbed the whiteboard off the counter. "I sure can't slip nothing by you, Loretta."

There was nothing like buttering up someone's already inflated ego.

"I could see right through you when I pranced right on in here a while ago." She nodded proudly.

I sat down on the edge of the hearth across from her and flipped the board around.

"A murder board," she gasped. "I've seen these on that British streaming station." She pinched off a corner of the bread and used it as a knife to spread the melted pat of butter around.

Evenly.

"I see you have Caspian and Danielle on there, which came right to my mind after I heard what happened, but do they really care the deal went south?" she asked, and I was all ears to listen. "Danielle will just go to the next job."

She had no idea, nor was it written on the board, about Leandar threatening to reveal Danielle's big secret.

"The Blackwood group has so many other dealings in different states that this is just a drop of money in the bucket for them." All the information rolled off her tongue, making me wonder how on earth she knew all of this already about them. "But the Featherstone family." She tsked. "That's a whole different kinda motive."

"How so?" I asked.

"I'm not gossiping, you know, but it was brought to my attention a few weeks ago at bunco. Jean Hill had told me Raffery Featherstone had put a stop on purchasing hay for the farm from her because he was selling," she said and then paused to pick up the cow creamer, slowly pouring the liquid into the coffee. "So she sold his hay plus any extra to other farmers. You know Jean Hill has some good hay." Loretta nodded.

Jean Hill was the owner of the local dairy farm. She had all sorts of things she sold that included items such as dairy, vegetables, flowers, and anything else she could grow. Her quality never suffered. She had the best homegrown vegetables I'd ever eaten. I made sure I used anything grown locally in all the dishes I made to sell at the Bean Hive.

"Wow. I guess Raffery was invested in moving." I took the moment to interject like I was shocked, too, not letting her know Aunt Maxi had already alerted me to the big estate sale they were going to have, which made me ask the next question. "What on earth are they going to do with all those treasures?"

In particular, I was wondering if Loretta had heard about the bone china.

She picked up the spoon I'd put on top of the napkin and slowly stirred.

"They did have an estate sale planned, and they've got a legal contract with Leandar for the sale of the house, but if he's"—she took the spoon and dragged it across her neck—"it would be null and void, I guess. The estate sale is tomorrow, right?"

"I think so." I had to remember to ask Aunt Maxi for sure. When she told me earlier today about the estate sale, it didn't seem to matter as much as it did now. "Where were the Featherstones going to live?" I asked her, thinking Leandar's murder had nothing to do with the country club.

I was wrong.

"The country club. Raffery was an investor. He had to sell the farm in order to invest." The more Loretta talked, the more I had to use the poker face I'd worn so many times in court when the prosecutor would throw me a curveball.

This was a curveball.

A game changer.

"He was going to have the best view of the lake, the million-dollar home with tiny square footage. From what I heard from Jean, he won't be able to get enough hay to keep the horses on the farm alive." Loretta nibbled on the bread. "It's too late in the season to get some at a reasonable price. I'm not sure if he can afford what he's going to need. So he's going to have to sell."

"What are you talking about?" I had lost whatever she thought I understood. "Break this down for me."

"Roxy, have you not been sleeping?" She swung her right leg over her left and clasped her hands together before she cradled her right knee. "Because you ain't following along at all."

"I'm sorry. I didn't get a lot of sleep last night, and then this morning when I saw the body..." I had to keep giving her little bits of information for her to want to give *me* information.

"You saw Leandar's body?" Her jaw dropped. She picked up the empty mug. "I'm gonna need a refill, so I can sip while you tell me all about it."

Loretta got up and helped herself to the coffee bar. She didn't slip any money in the convenience jar, but that was okay. Maybe the gift of her knowledge of the day's gossip would pay for the coffee.

"You mean to tell me he asked you to keep your ears peeled?" she asked after I told her about seeing Leandar and Spencer asking me to help.

She sat back down.

"He did, and my thoughts were on Caspian because Leandar's negligence is what got him here, but I never figured on other dealings Leandar had. I mean, it could be anyone he had a real estate agreement with or someone else." There was more to Leandar Taylor than met the eye.

The more I thought about it, the more I realized his fingers and hands were in a lot of people's pockets.

"You know Leandar," Loretta continued, thinking that I did know him. I didn't. I moved here as an adult, running a business. Most people here forgot I didn't grow up here, but I'd positioned myself for them to think I had. "He loves the almighty dollar, and we know that ain't good."

She let go of a deep and long sigh before she brought the cup to her lips, tipping it slightly to blow on the hot liquid before she took a sip.

"If anything, Raffery had so much more to lose. Did you see him rip up the plans last night after Danielle gave her presentation?" Loretta put the outburst in the forefront of my mind.

I'd been so fixated on the development, I'd not really taken into account that the entire group of citizens screaming how we needed to keep our land safe was probably directed more at Leandar than the development.

"Now that Leandar is dead, Raffery won't lose out on his millions. The only thing he's going to have to do, according to Jean, is find hay somewhere else to feed all those racing horses he was going to sell with the property." Loretta gave another little hint for an additional motive for Raffery to have killed Leandar. "But like I said, the hay will cost him a pretty penny, and I'm not sure he can afford it."

"He just might need to sell a racehorse or two," I held up two fingers and said, feeling like it was a pretty logical thing to do. But who was I to be logical?

I'd already made him a suspect and had an entire theory on why he was the killer. None of it was exactly logical, but it was enough to make me want to talk to him.

I updated the murder board after Loretta left, making a visit to Danielle and Raffery my first priority.

Underneath my newest suspect, Raffery Featherstone, I wrote down his motive to have killed Leandar Taylor.

"Raffery was going to sell his millions to invest in the new country club." I talked as I wrote the bullet points on the whiteboard. "It was a safe bet to say it would've been a great investment. We could use a golf course here."

I stepped back and looked at what I'd written. I took a sip of coffee and continued to think back to everything Loretta had said.

"With the development going under and the reaction Raffery had..." The look on Raffery's face came to my mind. The more I'd thought about his reaction to what Danielle had laid out, I wondered if she'd even told Caspian about it. "Did she drop the ball on him too?"

Both Caspian and Raffery had the look of a murderer on their faces. But Caspian was a businessman, and he'd probably been in this situation a time or two.

I quickly started to write Caspian's motive to murder Leandar.

"He had spent millions already on architecture plans. How much did Danielle charge him? And what about the investors? Who are they?" I tapped the end of the dry-erase marker on the board as I tried to figure out how I could get my hands on any documents.

The puppy had made his way over to the stool without me even hearing him until he stood next to the feet of the stool, whining.

"Hey, buddy. Do you need to go potty before we go?" I looked down at the cute puppy and popped off the stool.

The bell over the door dinged, and my afternoon employees stumbled in, giggling.

"Hey, Roxy!" the two greeted me. "Hey, Jessie!" They squealed and rushed over to grab the puppy.

Shanda and Shelley Riddle were twins who'd started working for me at the beginning of the year. They were in their junior year of high school, which made me believe they'd at least be here for the next couple of years before they went off to college.

"I'll take him out," Shanda said and darted out the door with the puppy.

"Jessie?" I asked, not knowing they'd named the dog.

"Yes. I think there might be someone who wants to adopt him. We have a regular who comes in at night to grab a decaf, and she said she's thinking about adopting him. She calls him Jessie." Shelley shrugged and headed on back to put her backpack away so she could start her work shift.

"What are you working on?" Shelley called out to me.

"Nothing." I grabbed the whiteboard and carried it with the backside facing out so she didn't see the words "murder" and "victim." "Just some recipes."

"For murder?" she asked and snickered. "Is that about that guy they found at the lake?"

"It's nothing for you to worry about," I said and pushed through the door of the kitchen so I could grab my things and head home.

I had so many questions I could look up on the internet, like who was investing into the country-club development. Plus, my mom hadn't called me back. I wanted to call her and ask her about all of these real estate dealings.

She would be able to steer me in the right direction.

"Hey!" I heard Shelley yell out, and it made me dart back through the swinging door. "That's Jessie's mom."

She pointed to the television we kept on the back wall with the sound down for those customers who liked to come watch the news in the morning while sipping on a coffee.

It was Danielle Quillen.

"Turn it up." I gestured for Shelley to grab the remote from underneath the counter.

We are looking for Ms. Quillen. We only want to talk to her. She worked with Leandar Taylor on the development where we found his body. We also have his phone, and she was the last person he called. We just want to talk to her.

Spencer Shepard was giving a quick television update with Danielle's face plastered all over the television.

"Do me a favor." I turned to Shelley and ripped my bag off the coatrack, forgetting about the stuff in the kitchen. "If she does come in tonight, call me. If not, make sure the puppy, er, Jessie is okay for the night."

My phone rang.

I waved goodbye to Shelley and hit the green button to answer my phone when I saw it was Mom.

CHAPTER SIX

"Hey, Mom. I guess you heard the news about Leandar," I said right off and unchained my bike from the bike rack in front of the shop.

"Yes. I was meaning to call you all day, but with the latest news, some of his clients have come to me after hearing. You know, the house-buying business doesn't stop for death." Mom really never had a good way with words.

She wasn't from the south or Kentucky, which already put her on Aunt Maxi's bad side. Mom didn't help herself, either.

My mom wasn't the typical mom when I was growing up, and Aunt Maxi was more of a mother figure, so it was natural for me to show up here years ago instead of going to find my mom who, at that time, was galivanting all over the world, God knows where.

It was the history between Aunt Maxi and Mom that was a difficult hurdle to jump through when Mom showed up in Honey Springs. When she decided to stay and call it home, it was just a little unnerving for me.

Mom didn't like it when my dad brought me here, and she certainly wasn't a fan when my dad would leave me here for the rest of the summer. Thankfully, he didn't listen to her, and I was able to stay, but still, the animosity was something she and Aunt Maxi had to work through.

I loved them both, but Mom was different. I had to give her credit. She had done what she set out to do, and that was create a new life with me in it as well as become a Realtor. She'd done well for herself. Aunt Maxi saw Mom was trying, and they'd come to a truce. If I had to make a comment about their relationship, I'd say they were more than friendly, and I'd like to think they'd call on one another if they were in a pickle.

"Did you happen to get a phone call from Danielle Quillen?" I asked and rolled the lock up to put in my bag before sticking it in the basket.

"Why would she call me?" Mom asked.

I held the bike steady with one hand, one foot on the pedal and my heinie resting on the seat while I finished the conversation.

"Because she was probably staying in one of Leandar's rentals." I made the assumption from deductive reasoning. If Blackwood Associates used him, it would seem natural that all the people they subcontracted out or employees would also use him.

"That's not true. He wanted an arm and a leg for a cabin that didn't even have a view of nothing but the old junkyard on the far side of town." Mom had a large clientele of owners who had not only bought old cabins from her, but after they'd redone them, they used Mom as their rental agent. "She came into the office, and I showed her the cabin over on the island with the perfect view of the property they were building on."

"You mean one of Kayla and Andrew's cabins?" I asked.

"Yes. She loves it, from what I understand. She'd extended her stay just a few days ago to two more months." Mom didn't make sense.

"You mean a month ago or at least a week or two ago, right?" I questioned the timing. If Danielle had gotten all her samples completed and now the project had all but come to an abrupt halt, especially now that it was a crime scene, why would she stay?

"No, honey. I said a couple of days ago," Mom confirmed. The distinctive sound of a filing cabinet clicking open and the small balls rolling along the rails was a sound I heard Mom make all the time when she was looking for a rental agreement or client file. It was followed by shuffling of papers. "Yep. It's right here. It was two days ago. And about the same time."

I pulled my phone away from my ear. It was almost four o'clock in the afternoon, which meant if I went to the marina, I could catch the four o'clock boat ride over to the bee farm and go see if Danielle was still at the cabin.

"Can you tell me which cabin?" I asked and decided to get off the bike, resting it up against the outside of the coffee shop so I could head inside to get some of the leftover donuts.

It was clear I was going to have to encounter some folks that weren't above donut bribes.

"Now, you know I can't do that. It's a privacy thing, but I did tell you it was directly across from the development." Mom sighed with satisfaction. "Why are you asking? You don't think she had anything to do with Leandar's murder, do you? I mean, there's so many other people I think would have motive. It wasn't like he was on the up-and-up with his shady real estate dealings."

The Riddle girls' brows knotted when they saw me come back in as they wondered what I was doing. They didn't ask as I hurried behind the counter and grabbed a few to-go bags and dumped donuts in them, putting them in my bag.

"What do you mean?" I asked and rushed back outside.

I put my bag back in the wire rack and started to walk the bike down the boardwalk. I had to make sure I caught the boat in time and heard what Mom had to say.

"Listen, honey. I have to go. I'm going to be late for the cruise the Featherstones paid for before the news of the development going south. I have to go home and get cleaned up." Mom was full of wonderful information.

"Cruise? You mean a dinner cruise at the Watershed?" I asked since it was the only local restaurant that offered such a thing.

"Roxanne Bloom." She only said my name when there was cause for concern. "Are you feeling okay?"

"I have a lot of questions about Leandar's death, and I can't help but wonder if Danielle or Raffery didn't have something to do with it." I rambled on. The low-pitched *thud* of the tires as they moved along the wooden planks of the boardwalk made it hard for me to concentrate.

"You mean to tell me Danielle and Raffery are a couple and they killed Leandar?" Mom had created a whole love triangle.

And this was how rumors started.

"No. Not at all." I had to stop the rumor train before it left the station. "You have to promise not to say a word," I told her and looked off toward the marina where I could see people getting on Big Bib's boat to hitch a ride over to the island.

"I promise." Mom didn't sound too convincing, but she did sound curious.

"I mean pinky promise. Like cross-your-heart-and-you'll-die if you don't keep it." I maneuvered the bike around some tourists down the ramp that led right to the marina. "That kind of promise."

"I promise, but I'm not sure I'm going to like it." Mom agreed enough for me to tell her about me seeing Leandar's body and how his skull had been bashed in, and I was sure he didn't do it himself. "Oh dear. Both Danielle and Leandar would have motives, plus Caspian Blackwood."

"Yes. And that's why I need to talk to Danielle. I also need to get in front of Raffery, which is why I wanted to know if you can take me as a guest to your cruise dinner they are hosting." I was a big ask for Mom to do this for me. "I know it's business for you, but there won't be business in the real estate market if it gets out there was a murder in town. No one wants to invest in crime-ridden communities."

The one thing I could count on with my mom was the power of the almighty dollar. It wasn't a good quality she had in her, but she looked at every transaction as a business deal. Leandar's murder was no different.

And I was using it as a way to get information. Yes.

"I was offered two tickets," she muttered as though she wasn't convinced I should go. She paused.

"Listen, I'm already at the marina to go find Danielle," I told her and handed my bike to Big Bib so he could put it somewhere for me until I got back from the island. "Thank you," I mouthed to him.

He winked.

"I'm stepping foot on the boat right now." This was when she knew I wasn't going to take "no" lightly, and I would do whatever I had to do to get on the cruise. "You know I will get on the cruise one way or the other, so you might'swell take me and save us both the embarrassment."

"Fine, but you can't go around asking if they murdered Leandar. I'm trying to get them to switch all of their property dealings to me, now that…" She didn't have to finish the sentence for me to know she was referring to Leandar's death.

"I'll meet you at the Watershed at… What time?" I asked and stepped down into the boat. I had limited time to talk. Soon I'd be surrounded by tourists and the hum of the motor of the boat as it crossed the lake, leaving me to talk loud, and I didn't want to risk anyone hearing me talk about murder.

"Be there at seven and wear a cocktail dress." Her words posed a problem, and before I could protest, she hung up.

I felt a mix of excitement and apprehension. The sun was beginning to dip lower in the sky, casting warm golden hues across Lake Honey Springs as we prepared to head toward the island. The late spring air was filled with the scent of blooming flowers and fresh grass while birdsong accompanied the gentle hum of the boat's engine.

"Ugh," I blurted out loud enough to catch Big Bib's attention as I tugged my bag in my lap.

"What was that about?" he asked, grinning underneath that heavy beard of his.

"Mom." I rolled my eyes. "I'm going to go as her guest on the dinner cruise tonight, and she told me I have to wear a cocktail dress. I don't have any. There's no need with slinging coffee and pastries all day."

He took his spot at the helm of the wheel boat, revving up the motor. I leaned on my hip and tugged my bag off my shoulder.

"Speaking of donuts," I said and put my hand down into my bag to pull out one of the to-go Bean Hive bags. "I thought you could use a couple after-supper dessert donuts."

His big beard couldn't hide the large grin on his face.

"You're butterin' me up, Roxanne Bloom." He gladly took the bag. "After supper, nothin'. I'm gonna eat these right now while you tell me what it is you want to know."

"You see a lot of people coming and going on this boat. Have you seen Danielle lately?" I asked in a casual tone.

Big Bib scratched his beard thoughtfully, his eyes never leaving the water ahead. "Well, Roxy," he said, "I did see her a couple of days ago. She seemed mighty upset, said she needed some time alone at her cabin on the island."

His hand gripped the handle, and he pushed it forward, accelerating the boat as it cut through the water, creating a gentle spray that misted my face. I looked around at the other passengers, who were chattering excitedly and snapping photos of the picturesque landscape. They were oblivious to the storm brewing beneath the surface of our seemingly peaceful community.

I bit my lip, mulling over this information. "Did she mention anything about Leandar or their argument at the Bean Hive?"

He shook his head. "No, but she did say she had some important information that she needed to sort through. Something that could change everything for this town. But that was before the town council, and we both know what happened there."

"Yeah. I'm going to go see if I can talk to her. See if she's okay. She'd been coming into the Bean Hive every day. Never missing once. She didn't show up today. Did you happen to give her a ride today?" I asked.

"No, but that doesn't mean someone else didn't." He shrugged.

"Like who?" I asked.

"I don't know. Look around." He nodded as the boat cut across the lake, missing other boats traveling downstream. "It's the beginning of boating season. I'm not the only ride someone can hitch back and forth. All the boat slips at the marina are all taken for the rest of the year. That means there's going to be a lot more boaters."

He pointed out to the dock we were headed for, and there were at least four boats tied up.

"Right there. Four boats. All of which are probably going to the resort." Bib had a point. "Speaking of which, you could ask Jessica for a dress."

"You're joking, right?" I asked, snorting to myself. But he didn't seem to laugh. "You're not."

"I'm just saying that woman has so many shopping bags when she comes from town, they are going to have to build a new resort just for her clothes." Bib laughed at his own joke.

Me, not so much.

My ex, Kirk, and his wife, Jessica, had been the secret investors for Crissy Lane's Be Happy Resort. It was a fancy spa and resort with all sorts of strange drinks like matcha or something that sounded icky. Plus all these crazy yoga classes that didn't sound like any kind of yoga or meditation I knew of.

When Crissy came back from California at some retreat, she got this harebrained idea to open something similar right smack-dab in Kentucky. Of course, we thought Crissy had lost her ever-lovin' mind, but who knew it would be so wildly popular and always packed after it was open?

It was quite a bit of a shock to find out my ex and his new wife had funded the place. To add insult to injury, they'd even moved to Honey Springs, now calling it home with their dog, who Jessica adopted from the Pet Palace. Biscuit. Cute feller. And now they had a newborn baby.

I didn't hold any grudges against either of them. They did contribute to society, but Kirk was a local lawyer, and I tried to stay as far away from them as possible.

Honey Springs wasn't that big, but it was big enough for me not to see them on a regular basis.

As we neared the island, I felt a knot forming in my stomach. Was

Danielle truly capable of murder? What secrets was she hiding? And what would I find when I confronted her?

The sun's golden rays began to fade, replaced by the soft pink hues of dusk. The scent of the lake and the sounds of nature surrounded us, but my thoughts were consumed by the mystery that lay ahead. I braced myself for the confrontation, determined to uncover the truth and protect the town I loved.

"So you don't recall Danielle ever saying anything about Leandar?" I asked Big Bib one more time after all the tourists had gotten off the boat.

"No, but I did hear Caspian Blackwood say if the nitwit Realtor didn't pull through with the deal, then it would be his last deal." Big Bib's observation wasn't one pointing to Caspian as the killer, but it was a situation I would ask Caspian about when I got in front of him.

There was a little itch of curiosity about who he'd been talking to.

"What time is the last ride back?" I asked Big Bib after I stepped off the boat onto the wooden dock, feeling the late-afternoon breeze brush against my face.

The air was filled with the sweet scent of honey and the sound of buzzing bees from the honey farm behind me.

"I'll be back here in about an hour." His eyes lowered. "Do I need to come looking for you if you don't show up?" He shook his head. "I'm always wondering about you."

"You just might." I smiled, referring to his offer to come look for me. "Can I get you anything from the bee farm?"

"I don't think he needs anything." Kayla Noro had crept up behind me. "We just gave him two big honey pots yesterday."

"Hey!" I was happy to see Kayla. It was a long winter, and I'd yet to get over there that spring.

Though the island was literally a Big Bib pontoon boat ride away from land, it did seem like it was a trip. Like most things, Kayla and Andrew had their hands full with taking care of all the bees and hives in order to keep them healthy for the popular tourist farm.

"I'm so glad to see you." Kayla tucked her elbow in the crook of my arm.

We walked off the dock and headed up the cute little path toward the bee farm.

"I have loved getting to visit with Maxine. She's never gonna change." Kayla shook her head. "The older she gets, the worse she gets."

"You're not telling me anything. But I'm glad she's been able to get over here to get my supply of honey." I sighed, thinking how grateful I was for Aunt Maxi's involvement in the Bean Hive.

She really was someone who thought I could do anything.

"I'm glad you came here and not there." Kayla's eyes shifted toward the Be Happy Spa that was located on the opposite end of the island.

It was a piece of property Kayla and Andrew sold off to Crissy and her investors after the bee farm had taken a hit. Seasonal weather sometimes took a toll on the bees' health, and the Noros didn't have enough funds to keep the hives open, keep the bees healthy, and make a living unless they sold some land.

"No, but I am glad it's all going good over there. Crissy sure does love all that woo-woo stuff. I'm here to try to find one of the rental cabins." That was another business deal the Noros had done during their time of need.

They'd not sold off land, but they'd built a couple of cabins so they could rent them for income. I'd never seen them, but I knew they rented them, and Mama told me Danielle was currently renting one of them from the Noros.

"Oh." Kayla pulled her arm from mine.

"Yeah. Danielle Quillen." As I said her name, Kayla's facial expression changed considerably. "I can see you've heard about Leandar."

"It's awful, and immediately I thought about the last time I saw him." Her lips tugged in as though she wasn't sure she wanted to let out whatever it was she was itching to tell me.

"If you know something, please tell me." I blinked at her before I told her, "Spencer asked me to keep my ear to the ground, and you know what that means."

"Yeah. I hate to spread rumors or gossip." She shook her head, still unsure if she wanted to tell me what she knew.

"It wasn't too long ago that I helped you and Andrew." I didn't want to throw it in her face. "Since I'm still a lawyer, I might be able to help Danielle."

"I wondered if she was a suspect in Leandar's murder after I heard about the emergency meeting at All About the Details." When Kayla sucked in a deep breath, her shoulders lifted to her ears and suddenly dropped as her mouth opened. "He came to the island looking for her. He seemed quite upset and muttered something about her past. He was determined to find her and said he wouldn't leave until he did."

"Did he find her?" I asked.

"No. I told him she wasn't here and how she'd taken the ferry." She used "ferry" loosely when we were actually talking about Big Bib's pontoon. It was the only official ride over to the island.

"Did he go look for her?" I wanted to know.

"Not on the island. I told him she always took the first ferry off the island and usually stopped by the Bean Hive." She pointed to me. "He jumped back on the ferry, but he was determined to find her." Kayla frowned.

"When was this?" I asked.

"Yesterday morning," she said, placing him at the Bean Hive about the time I'd overheard him threaten Danielle.

"Do you think I need to tell Spencer?" she asked.

"I probably would. He's asking for anyone with any information to come forward, and there's nothing too small. All clues add up," I said. "Like you said, Danielle does come to the coffeehouse every morning, but she didn't show up today."

Kayla's face elongated as her eyes bolted open and her jaw dropped.

"That's why I'm here. I have a few questions for her and can possibly be able to help her." It was my way of reminding Kayla I was still a lawyer and used it to my advantage. "Can you tell me what cabin she's staying in?"

"You'll find her cabin just beyond the old oak tree over there," she said, pointing toward a massive tree in the distance. "There are a couple, but the one she rented…" She paused then said, "Extended her rental recently." She followed her comment by saying, "If she killed someone, then she's probably taken off. Right?"

"Not necessarily." My lips tugged apart in a grimace. "Either they run or they hang around to see what people know."

"Oh." Kayla tugged her bottom lip under her front teeth. She closed her eyes and shook her head. "I can't even imagine her doing something like this."

"Me either. That's why I want to talk to her before Spencer tries to arrest her or take her in for questioning."

"I didn't see her this morning. Not that I look, but she usually has Big Bib pick her up just as the sun is popping up and my bees need to be checked while I'm drinking my homemade cup of coffee from the Bean Hive special roast." She made me smile.

I pointed off in the direction of the big tree.

"Yep. Hers is the one on the beach," Kayla said. "Stop by before you head back over. I'll give you some fresh honey I collected today. It's so sweet."

"I will, but before I go find her, did you happen to see Caspian Blackwood, the development owner, here?" I asked since Big Bib had told me he'd overheard Caspian on the phone.

"No. He's never been here." She shook her head with confidence. "He could've killed Leandar. Can you imagine all the money he's out? I know when Crissy and Kirk—" She pulled her lips together. "Sorry," she apologized.

"Don't be. It's fine. I've moved on, if you've not heard," I teased, holding up my ring finger, since she was one of the first people to congratulate me during our annual Neewolah Festival, where Patrick and I tied the knot without telling anyone.

"Good," she sighed. "Kirk did pay for all the environmental things we had to do in order for them to build the spa, and let me tell you, I got a gander at the figures on a piece of paper when we were we meeting with him, and they were staggering. So I'm sure Blackwood Associates is out a pretty penny."

"Danielle Quillen might've been hiding some secret Leandar knew about and she didn't want him to reveal, but was it enough to kill him to shut him up?" I asked myself because I wasn't sure.

"What? A secret?" Kayla looked shocked. "What kind of secret?"

"That is the million-dollar question and why I'm going to go find Danielle to ask," I said. "Now that you mention the money that it took for just the environmental inspection of the spa, Caspian Blackwood had invested a lot—if not millions—on making this country-club development community come to life, and all the money he's spent so far is money that doesn't come with a return policy."

"No, siree, it's not returned," Kayla repeated. "And money is a big stick in the gut, and when you lose a lot of it, it can make you crazy."

"Crazy enough to kill?" I asked.

Kayla slowly nodded her head and said, "Enough if it's a lot of money and currently the only project you're banking on to bring you to early retirement."

"Early retirement?" I was beginning to think Kayla knew more than she was telling me.

"I wasn't going to say anything because, well, Kirk." Kayla frowned and gave me an empathetic look. "You said winters are long, and...", she hesitated.

"You and Kirk and Jessica have gotten to be friends," I finished for her.

"Yes. And Jessica is lovely. She's so sweet, and Kirk is so smart about business. He and Andrew clicked. It's been nice. Not lonely, and it gives me and Andrew more than just each other to talk to." Kayla was making a good argument for why they were friends.

"Truth be told, I liked Jessica the day she came into the coffeehouse, not telling me who she was and immediately adopting Biscuit. If she wasn't tied to Kirk, I would say we'd be friends too." My words landed on Kayla like a breath of fresh air.

"Thank you." She put her hands together up to her third eye. "We will always be better friends."

"You don't have to go that far." I assured her. "Are you telling me Kirk mentioned something about Caspian?"

"Yes. Of course, when he heard about the development, he said he wondered why he'd not thought of it first and was mad. Then he told us how he went to Blackwood Associates to talk to Caspian. Later, Jessica told me Kirk went there to see if he could become one of the investors." I was all ears about their little get-togethers. "That's when Caspian told Kirk he'd put all his money into this one development because he was planning on moving here to retire. All of his money. Like every single penny."

"Did Kirk invest?" I asked.

"Yes." Kayla nodded. "A lot, according to Jessica. After what happened at the meeting yesterday, I called her, and she said she couldn't talk. Things weren't good at home."

"Wow." I wasn't expecting to have this big bombshell laid out on me. I only had limited time to talk to Danielle and get back on the ferry ride home, but while I was there, I wanted to pop into the spa and maybe have a little chat with my dear old ex-husband.

"I better get going if I'm going to stop back by and grab some of that fresh, sweet honey." I waved off to her and hurried toward the oak tree, now more concerned than ever about Danielle's safety rather than her being a suspect.

What if Caspian was getting rid of everyone who'd made the deal go south?

The island's serenity suddenly seemed to fade as the reality of the situation set in. With determination in my step, I continued weaving through the bee farm, eager to reach Danielle and uncover the secrets that seemed to haunt her.

CHAPTER SEVEN

On my way to find Danielle's cabin, I couldn't help but try to fit going to see Kirk in my schedule while I was on the island. It wasn't like I was going to be able to solve this thing tonight—that wasn't the question.

The question was if I could force myself to not scratch the curious itch I had.

There was a huge difference in the landscape as I stepped off the property line of the bee farm and into what I'd consider more inhabited land.

A soft breeze kissed my face, carrying the sweet scent of honey and the faint buzzing sound of bees hard at work. The sun was shining brightly, casting a warm golden hue over the verdant landscape that stretched before me before it would soon set. I couldn't help but feel an overwhelming sense of serenity, as if Mother Nature herself was hugging me.

No wonder Crissy thought the island would be a great place for the Be Happy Spa. It felt like you were in a different part of the world. Just far enough away from the mainland to give you a sense of awe.

I began to walk toward the island beach, following a well-trodden path that weaved through tall grasses and wildflowers. The earth beneath my feet was damp from the recent rain, making a satisfying squelching sound with each step I took. I inhaled the sweet fragrance of freshly blossomed flowers. The chirping of birds filled the air, creating a beautiful symphony that accompanied me on my journey.

As I continued along the path, I could feel the ground beneath my feet becoming sandier, signaling that I was nearing the beach. My thought was to walk toward the big oak like Kayla had suggested, but if I found the beach and walked it, there was no way I could miss the cabin Danielle had rented.

The sound of gentle waves lapping at the shore replaced the buzzing of bees, and the fresh scent of the lake air mixed with the lingering sweetness of honey. I paused for a moment to take in the picturesque view of the crystal-clear lake, its surface sparkling like a thousand diamonds under the sun's rays.

I could see the small cabin nestled in the trees, its wooden structure blending harmoniously with the surrounding foliage. The leaves rustled gently in the breeze, creating a soothing background melody that further added to the enchanting atmosphere.

As I approached the cabin, I felt the sand beneath my toes grow warmer, and I could hear the faint voice I'd recognized as Danielle echoing out of the small cabin. That's when I knew it was, in fact, her cabin.

Finally, I reached the cabin's door, which was slightly ajar, allowing the warm, inviting light from within to spill out onto the sandy path. I knocked gently and called out Danielle's name, the sound of my voice mingling with the symphony of nature that surrounded us.

"I've got to go," I heard her say in a whisper.

"Danielle? It's Roxy from the Bean Hive," I called again. "I missed you today."

There was no movement or sound of movement coming from inside.

"I wanted to talk to you about Leandar." There was no beating around the bush. "Actually, I'm guessing you know that I overheard him mention something about exposing you, then we had the emergency meeting where he wasn't happy, and now he's dead. Not that I'm accusing you, but it doesn't look all that great, and well, I'm a lawyer."

The door went from cracked to fully open with Danielle standing behind it, her hand on the doorknob.

"You're a lawyer?" she asked. There was almost a look of relief on her face. Just for a split second. Still, there was an opening for me.

"I brought donuts." I dug down into my bag and pulled out the sack, dangling it in front of her.

"Is it too late for coffee?" she asked with a simple smile. "It's not your coffee, but it's coffee."

"I love all coffee." I held out the bag. "Want to talk?"

She opened the door to the small cabin, gesturing a welcome to come inside.

As I stepped inside the cabin, I was immediately greeted by a sense of warmth and comfort. The interior was a perfect blend of rustic charm and modern convenience, with exposed wooden beams criss-crossing the ceiling and polished hardwood floors that creaked ever so softly beneath my feet. Natural light filtered through the large windows, casting a warm glow that illuminated the cozy space.

To my left, a small-yet-functional kitchenette occupied one corner of the cabin. It featured a compact refrigerator, a gas stove, and a sink with a window above it that offered a beautiful view of the lake. The wooden countertops and open shelves were adorned with colorful ceramic dishes and a collection of well-loved cookware, telling the story of countless shared meals and laughter-filled gatherings.

A comfortable living area occupied the center of the cabin, with a plush sofa draped in soft, patterned throws and an array of mismatched cushions. A vintage coffee table sat on a woven rug, boasting a stack of dog-eared books and a simple vase filled with fresh wildflowers. On one wall, a stone fireplace. I imagined how cozy and warm it would feel in here during the winter.

To my right, a small wooden ladder led to a lofted sleeping area with a low, slanted ceiling. The space was adorned with a cozy bed dressed in soft linens and a patchwork quilt that looked as though it had been lovingly handmade. A small round window in the loft allowed a gentle breeze to waft through the cabin, carrying with it the sweet scent of the surrounding nature.

Throughout the cabin, personal touches were evident in the form of framed photographs, hand-painted artwork, and other mementos that spoke of cherished memories and shared experiences. Every corner of the space exuded a sense of warmth and love, making it feel like a true home away from home.

"Wow. Kayla has really made this a great little hideaway." It was as almost as cute as my home.

"They've been great. I can't complain." She busied herself in the small kitchen, making a single-serve coffee from the maker and plating the donuts. "Would you like one?"

"No. I don't want to ruin my supper. I'm going as a guest of my mama's to the Featherstones' dinner cruise." I patted my belly. "If I can get a free meal, I'm saving the room in my stomach. But I'll always have a coffee."

"I was invited to it, until I wasn't." She sat down at the kitchen table for two and bit into the donut.

"They uninvited you?" I wanted to make sure what I thought she was saying was correct and not assumptive.

"Right after the emergency meeting, Raffery was outside looking for Leandar, and I crossed his path at the wrong time." She shook her head. "He was fuming about the development. He said Leandar should've known better and that I ruined everything. That's when he pointed at me and told me to just pack my things and get out of town. He followed it up by saying, 'You are not welcome at the dinner cruise.'"

"I'm sorry. I bet that was hurtful." I frowned and held up my hand when I noticed the first cup of coffee had brewed. "You sit. I'll get our coffees."

"Thank you," she whispered and looked down at what was left of the first of the two donuts. "There's creamer in the refrigerator."

With the creamer in one hand and the cup in the other, I placed them in front of her then went back to make myself a cup of coffee.

"I understand I'm the bad guy here." She dunked the donut in the steaming coffee. My kinda girl, I thought to myself. "The town was counting on the country club to not only provide jobs but also bring in more tourism. I let everyone down."

"You didn't. I think it's a great idea for a nature preserve like you suggested. You even went above and beyond with Alice Dee Spicer to implement something. I think tourists come to Honey Springs for the nature. Lake Honey Springs is the big draw." The cup of coffee finished brewing, and I walked over to sit across from Danielle. "When a tourist comes to Honey Springs and puts a photo on social media, nine out of ten times, the photo is something in nature. A fish they saw in the lake, a bird nesting along the beach, a crazy purple insect native to the area."

Her eyes were filled with tears as what I was saying seemed to have an effect on how she was starting to see it wasn't her fault.

"Those are the things you love. That's why you became an environmentalist, right? To protect lands but also be fair to those big developers who want to use land that's not going to hurt the landscape." Goodness, I sure was making a good case. Too bad it wasn't in front of a judge and jury.

"Now you sound like a lawyer." It was if she were reading my mind.

"No. I'm trying to be a friend who doesn't want her friend to beat herself up." I reached across the table and patted her wrist. "I admit, I came here to question you and see if you did kill Leandar. But I know you didn't."

"How do you know that?" she asked, with more relief on her face.

"I have a good way of reading people. It's my gift that helped me win a lot of cases, and I don't think you did it. But I also know Sheriff Spencer Shepard will want to question you after he gets the crime scene cleared and evidence collected. You will be first on his list." My words didn't sit well.

"I didn't do it. You just said you didn't think I did either." The frail-young-woman look had been replaced by determination.

"That's the attitude and look you need to have on your face at all times." I pointed it out to her. "And if you want to answer some key questions for me right now, I can take those to Spencer so they won't waste their time checking you out."

"I have nothing to hide," she stated emphatically.

"I think you do." I picked up the coffee and took a sip, leaving some space for my response to settle on her.

It was a technique we'd learned in law school, how sometimes dangling a carrot and then saying nothing gets you the answer much faster. No one ever liked silence anymore. It was an art to forcibly keep your mouth shut in most social situations these days. The silence made the other person uncomfortable, which by nature, made them open their mouths to talk.

"You're referring to what Leandar said to me in the Bean Hive." She was a smart girl. She knew she was going to have to tell me. "I've not always been as virtuous as it appears. A few years back, I consulted for a major corporation on an eco-friendly project. I was new in the field, and I had rent to pay."

It became clear this had to do with money, making her motive look even worse.

"I overlooked some harmful environmental practices to keep the client happy and secure a hefty paycheck for myself. If this information were to become public, it could severely damage my reputation and jeopardize my career. People might think twice about hiring me."

She ran her finger along the top of her mug. The silence had gotten even thicker than before, as I tugged my lips a little more to make sure not to say anything.

"It wasn't illegal, what I'd done. It was immoral, and I paid for it. The money I made was spent on years of therapy trying to come to terms with what I'd done." She'd pretty much put herself in her own jail over it. I didn't need to beat her up anymore. "That's when I started to really take a look at the other jobs and do more research while on those jobs. Just like this one. I could easily have incorporated that spring into a feature for the country club, but that doesn't make it right for the environment down the road."

"Even though I don't think you killed Leandar to silence him, I do need to know where you were and who you were with from the time you saw Raffery Featherstone to when you heard about what happened to Leandar."

She nodded and picked up the other donut, dunking it before she took a bite.

"That's easy." She looked away, over at the bag I'd seen her carry into the Bean Hive. The one with all her files. "I have receipts for the spa at Be Happy and drinks at the bar."

"Did you talk to anyone while you were there?" I knew it could be easy to get receipts. Not that I thought Danielle would do that or be so forward-thinking.

Let's face it—who took paper receipts anymore? I always told the cashiers to throw my receipt away, leaving an establishment without one. It was safe to say they would throw those in the trash, making it easy for someone who needed an alibi to root through the trash and find receipts for a time stamp that put them there around the times in questions.

"Yes. The owner's wife." She got up, stuffing the rest of the donut in her mouth.

"Crissy doesn't have a wife," I blurted out.

"Jessica, um…" She searched for the name.

"Ah. Jessica." I snorted, raising my chin. "Jessica is married to my ex-husband." There was a shocked look on Danielle's face when she turned to hand me the receipts. "We all have secrets."

"I'm sorry. She was very nice. I didn't meet your ex, but she was actually walking the beach after the meeting. I was sitting on the small dock." Danielle turned to look out the window.

"I didn't see that coming up." I noticed there was a little boat tied up. "Have you used the boat to go to the mainland?"

"Yes. It's not easy, but I figured it out. The development is right across the way, and when I saw all the flashing lights there, I thought someone had went over there and, I don't know, cut down some trees, trashed it." She shrugged. "Anyways, Jessica was walking the beach, and she recognized me from the meeting."

"Yes. They were investors for the development." I saw a look indicating that something had clicked in her brain.

"That's how she knew all about it." Danielle shook her head and sat back down. I looked at the receipts while she talked. "She asked me if I wanted to come back for a spa treatment at half price since they had a last-minute cancellation. I really needed it, so I took her up on her offer."

There was something fishy going on with all of this, but I wasn't sure what, so I let her keep talking.

"She even waited for me in the lobby of the spa. She said she wanted to know if her husband could use the boat to run across the lake to get their dog some food because there wasn't a ferry running. I told her I had some hot dogs back at the cabin for the dog, but she insisted the dog needed special food. I didn't see any harm in it, so I told her to tell him sure and that the keys were always left in the boat." The more she talked, the more her story played in my head like a television show. "Then she asked me if I wanted to have a drink at the bar, on the house, and I said I sure could use that too. So I did."

"When did you get back to the cabin?" I was trying to see if she knew if Kirk had used the boat or not.

"In the morning. Early. I had a little too much to drink, and Jessica let me stay in one of the rooms at the spa. I woke up disoriented, really early, before dawn, and that's when I walked back to the cabin and saw all the lights. But, like I said, I figured it was someone trashing the place, mad about what I'd discovered and said at the meeting."

"Let's go back to Caspian Blackwood." I had to get off the subject of Kirk, or I wouldn't be able to keep my cool. The man had always been motivated by money, and I had a lot of stories that could implicate him in a lot of murders he'd clearly not done, but still.

Danielle's encounter with Jessica didn't look good.

"Did you ever hear him say anything about Leandar that would give him motive to have killed him?" I asked.

"The money alone. Greed," Danielle spit out immediately. "My report wasn't wrapped up into the package deal he had with his investors. They didn't want the report done, but Caspian did. My cost alone was over sixty thousand dollars. Then he had all the other contractors out there. Even though they'd yet to pluck a piece of grass off the land, their time isn't cheap, especially when Blackwood Associates had to fly them in, which isn't easy." She snorted. "Then get them rooms to stay in. Not cheap."

"Were they paying for your cabin?" I asked.

"Yes, until a day or so ago. I went to the Realtor and re-signed a lease, knowing I'd have to be here for some questioning. It was easier to stay here than try to find something new." She told me all the answers I needed for now.

"I've overstayed. I don't even think I will make it back to the dock to catch the ferry." I jumped up after I saw the time.

"Take the dinghy boat." She pointed out the window. "It is right across the road from my house." It was a great idea, but the beach where they found Leandar wasn't high on my list of places to visit. "It would be convenient. Are you sure you won't need it until tomorrow?"

"No. I've got a good book over there to read. One of those cozy mysteries." She chuckled. "I think I'll just hole up here until I have to go talk to the sheriff."

"I can take you there tomorrow, and I'll even write up your statement." I didn't want to encourage her to go without me. Was it for her? Or was it for Kirk's sake?

I knew I could get Danielle's alibi to stick and she wouldn't be a suspect, but my mind took me to a place I certainly didn't want to go. No matter how fast I throttled the boat across the water to the development so I could cross the street to get back to my house, the new suspect in my head wasn't going away.

What if Kirk and Jessica knew Danielle was staying? They had kept Danielle occupied while Kirk took the boat over to the development. It would be like Kirk to call Leandar and get him to meet Kirk there and get his take on what Danielle said just so they could come up with a creative solution. The boat skidded up on the beach, and I jumped out to pull it up on shore, looking back across at where I'd come from.

Kirk could've easily gotten into this boat and across Lake Honey Springs without anyone seeing him. Would Jessica take part in something like that?

The last little bit of sun was visible before it started to fully set as I gave the boat one more tug to secure it on the beach, so it didn't float away until I could safely get it back to the island later.

"What is that?" I noticed something red on the edge of the boat. On closer inspection, I could clearly see what looked to be a bloody outline of a hand. I gulped. "Oh, Kirk."

CHAPTER EIGHT

We weren't expecting any more rain after last week's downpour, but I still didn't want to take any chances, so I snapped a few quick photos of the edge of the boat before I darted off into the woods between the beach and the road to cross to my house.

It was so hard to keep quiet about the bloody handprint I'd seen on the boat. The dinghy was safe, and no one but Danielle knew it was there. I wasn't about to skip the dinner cruise, even though the bloody handprint was enough evidence for me to safely say Kirk had been in contact with blood the night he'd schlepped across the lake on his secret, covert mission.

When I saw him at the dinner cruise, it was nearly impossible for me to keep my mouth shut, so I made sure I stuffed it with some crab cakes from the tray one of the serving staff was floating around.

"Tell me again why you were invited here." My hand grabbed a flute of champagne when the drink tray passed by.

"When the development went through, I saw an opportunity, and I took it." Leave it to Mama to find a loophole in a bad situation that she could turn around for the good. "That's Raffery Featherstone."

She pointed across the dining room to the man I recognized from the meeting.

"They are a big family, and if you know anything about them, you know they have a lot of racehorses on their property. I know a lot of people who knew he was going to be in a pickle," she ho-hummed, waving across the room to him.

He returned the wave with a smile and gestured for her to come over.

"I knew the deal was going south fast when Leandar Taylor came into the office a couple of days ago, saying the environmentalist was ruining everything. He wanted to know if I had any clients with lake-front property—and lots of it—they'd sell for a pretty penny." She led the way through a much larger crowd than I'd expected to see at the dinner cruise.

I'd thought it was for family, but apparently not. There were a lot of business owners I'd recognized, like the Teagardens and Alice Dee Spicer, plus Kirk.

"You're telling me Leandar was going around trying to get some land to get Blackwood Associates to look at after the natural spring was found?" I asked Mama, trying to keep up as we darted across the room.

"That natural spring was found about a week ago. It's just taken that long for the report to come back with all the findings." She planted a big smile on her face as soon as she stepped in front of Raffery. "Hello, Raffery. Thank you so much for inviting me. Let me introduce you to my plus-one. My daughter, Roxanne Bloom."

No one ever used my married name Cane.

I peeked around her shoulder and extended my arm around her to shake his hand. She wanted to be front and center.

"This is my son, Caldwell Featherstone. He got home today from college. He was going to help out with the estate sale that's not ever going to happen." Raffery groaned his disdain for the situation. "But we are all here to celebrate something, right?"

"That's right." Mama continued to smile, keeping her eyes on Raffery. "I have some really good news."

"We don't have to do business here." He tried to stop her.

"This we will celebrate." Mama sucked in a deep breath and let it go, saying, "I have secured a year's worth of hay for the same amount you paid last year from a farm over in Versailles."

"That is something to celebrate!" Raffery held his glass up in the air. "Ladies and gentlemen." His voice boomed across the room.

Everyone fell silent, and all eyes were on us.

"If you've not met Penny Bloom, you want to. She's done the unthinkable or unimaginable for this time of the year." He laid a proud hand on Mama's shoulder. "Not only is she a real estate agent but she went above and beyond to secure some hay for my horses for the next year at the same cost of what I paid last year. Isn't that great? Three cheers for Penny!"

The hear-hears trickled across the room before the captain of the dinner cruise came across the loudspeakers, letting us know they were pushing back from the dock at the Watershed and saying if anyone had any reason not to continue on, they should get off the boat now.

"That's a big deal your mom has done." Caldwell came up to me after Mama had ventured off with Raffery.

She was doing exactly what she'd come here to do.

Be introduced.

"Please be sure to let her know we really are grateful." Caldwell stood at least five feet, ten inches, with a lean, athletic build. He had a mop of wavy chestnut-brown hair long enough for him to tuck behind his ears, giving me a sense of a somewhat carefree appearance.

His deep-set hazel eyes conveyed a mixture of intensity and intelligence, while his strong jawline and slightly crooked smile lent him an air of approachability and made him very likable, unlike the feeling I got about his father.

Raffery, on the other hand, was well-put-together and, though my mom couldn't see it, I could tell by the way the man looked at her, and even at his own son, that he had a sense of indignation and would much rather be somewhere else now that the deal was dead in the water. Or should I have said, now that the Realtor was found dead in the water?

His Realtor. The one he could've killed.

"What are you studying in college?" I made small talk with Caldwell, who definitely had not dressed according to the dress code Penny had given me.

His wrinkled khakis were paired with a simple, well-fitted T-shirt. What looked like a trusty pair of worn-in sneakers finished off the outfit.

He definitely didn't have his father's buttoned-up style, and maybe that was what made him more approachable and really down-to-earth.

"I'm an education major. I want to be a physical-education teacher," he told me, which was exactly what his physique had told me. "Now, my dad, he wanted me to go into business. He said I could take over all of his dealings." He shook his head. "I don't need a business degree to say the investment he made with that country club was too much."

"Yeah." I frowned. "I guess you heard about that. I mean, my mom and all." I pointed out the little toast Raffery just gave in Mom's honor.

I noticed the server passing by and stopped him.

"Would you like a drink?" I offered one to Caldwell as I plucked another one for me.

"I'm twenty," he said flatly. "And I don't drink because I try to live the way I want to teach people how to treat their bodies."

"Sounds good." I plucked another one for me, making it one in each hand. "My ex is here, and..." My eyes narrowed, staring at Caldwell. He didn't give two iotas about me or Kirk. So I changed the subject. "Now, I guess you won't be moving."

"I don't live here. I came in town a couple of days ago to help get all the estate-sale items together." He had said something that stuck in my head.

"Couple of days ago?" I asked before turning to the people next to me. "Do you want a drink?" I offered them the flutes of champagne, knowing if I drank them, I couldn't be sure what I would say to Kirk. If I was going to accuse him of murder, then I better be in tip-top lawyer form because he'd be nothing less.

"Yeah. We are on summer break. I work a few summer camps at the local schools where I go to college. Mom wanted me to help out by going through things I might want, but there's nothing I want." He stuffed his hands in his pockets. "I guess we don't have to worry about that now."

"Yeah. That was bad. I mean, the other night, your dad was pretty upset about the real estate guy that died," I whispered out of the corner of my mouth. No matter what I did, I wasn't cool. So I just came out and said it. "What did you and your dad do after the meeting?"

"He was mad, and when he gets mad, it's best he goes fishing. We keep a boat down at the marina." Had Caldwell just told me his dad had gone fishing?

"Fishing? At night?" I asked.

"Jug fishing." He mentioned a type of fishing I knew well. One that you only did at night. Well, you put the jugs out at night.

He continued, "I even cut the fishing wire and hooked the end of the line as he tied them on the new milk jugs. You should've seen his old ones." He snickered.

He was talking about how you tie one end of the fishing line to the mouth of an empty milk jug, then you let the line dangle down into the water with the hook on it. The milk jug will float until a fish eats the bait and gets the hook in their mouth. The jug stands straight up in the water and zigzags around the lake all night.

"What color did he paint his jugs?" I asked because mine were painted purple, so when I went to get my jugs the next morning, I could find mine.

"His are red."

"Red," I repeated to remember to go look for red jugs, though he should've gone to get them by now.

"You didn't go with your dad?" I asked.

"Nope. He was gone all night. Well, I think he got in around four." He put his dad at the scene.

"In the morning?" I asked.

"Yes. Why?" He laughed like I said something funny.

"I didn't think anyone but me was up at that time." I shrugged so he wouldn't catch on to me snooping. "I own a coffee shop on the boardwalk."

"That's where I've seen you." He pointed at me. A look of "aha!" came up on his face. "I was in one of the home economics classes you talked to at Honey Springs High School."

"Oh. I'm sorry. I was so nervous that I barely looked at the kids." It was my way of being nice, but honestly, I never remembered seeing him. "While you're in town, you should come by and see me. Coffee on the house."

"I will. I'd love to have one of your famous maple-bacon coffees." He mentioned the most ordered drink for kids his age. "I'm not sure how long I'll be in town now that the estate sale isn't going to happen."

"You get one large maple-bacon coffee on the house. If I'm not there, you tell them to call me." I was interrupted by the loudspeaker as it screeched on and the captain let us know the dinner buffet was open for everyone to get a plate and enjoy the food.

"Are you sure your dad came in around four a.m.?" I asked before I scooted toward the dining room.

He confirmed it and said he was playing his online video game when his dad popped into his room to see why he was still awake.

Great. Now how was I going to be able to place Raffery at the scene without making his son a witness?

CHAPTER NINE

As the guests filled in the room to find their name at the place they'd be sitting, the captain gave little bits and pieces of information about Honey Springs as we passed various sites. He was talking about the island and how the bee farm was a tourist destination, pointing out how some of the decorations for the night's cruise were donations from the Noros.

I glanced around the dining area to see what Kayla had put together and noticed how the gorgeously adorned chandeliers dangling over the room cast a warm golden glow over the white linen-covered tables.

It was the centerpieces of each table that had Kayla's signature look. Stunning bouquets of flowers, reminiscent of the unique flora that contributed to the island's famous honey.

The chatter of guests filled the room, but the underlying tension was palpable.

I gripped the handle of the chair in front of the place setting with my name inscribed on the tented nameplate that sat on the fine piece of bone china. At a closer glance, I wondered if it was the famous Featherstone bone china I was going to see if I could get a few pieces of at the estate sale.

"If you're wondering"—Mama came up behind me—"because I saw

your mind going a million miles a minute when you looked at the plate, it is the family china. Raffery thought it would be a nice touch to have the farewell cruise include the china before they sold it at the estate sale."

I snorted and tried not to look across the table when Kirk appeared in my peripheral vision. Instead, I focused on the waitstaff, dressed in crisp white shirts and black bow ties, navigating the room with practiced grace and offering flutes of champagne and various wines to go with the dinner buffet. The scent of the gourmet dishes being prepared in the galley wafted through the air, making my stomach rumble in anticipation.

"Gotta go to my seat." Mama patted my back before she waved at someone else she knew and darted off to find her spot.

"Roxy." Kirk gave me a hard nod from across the table.

"Roxanne," I corrected him. "Roxy is reserved for my friends."

He smiled, picked up his glass of water, and tilted it toward me, then took a drink.

"Sorry. It's just I want to know why you were on the dinghy the night Leandar was murdered," I whispered hastily so no one else could hear me and tapped on my phone to bring up the photo I'd taken of the fingerprints of blood on the dinghy boat. "And you left this bloody handprint."

In the back of my head, I also kept the jug-fishing story Caldwell had told me about Raffery and how he'd used red paint to distinguish his jugs from the others floating on top of the lake.

"What are you talking about?" Kirk looked offended, his fork in one hand and his knife in the other. He used his knife to part the flower arrangement so he could glare at me. "What dinghy?"

"The dinghy boat from the cabin Kayla and Andrew rented to Danielle Quillen. The woman you and your wife used as an alibi for what you've done." I pushed the flowers aside so we had a clear path for our accusations and war of words to fly across without any sort of obstacle in the way.

"Outside." He grabbed the napkin from his lap and tossed it on the table. "Now," he said before he shoved his chair back from the table and got up.

"Excuse me," I said to the woman next to me who had noticed the little bit of tension between me and Kirk. "My ex. We have some issues to work out."

Why I had a need to apologize to the woman was beyond me, and I beat myself up over it in my head during the entire walk outside from the dining area where I found Kirk next to the boat's railing.

"What on earth is going on with you, Roxy? You've lost your mind if you think I had anything to do with Leandar's murder, but to accuse Jessica is going over the line." He stuck his finger in my face. "Even for you."

"Move your finger from my face," I said in a very nice tone. "Are you telling me Danielle lied to me about last night's little spa-and-bar romp, and her receipts with the time stamp are fudged?"

"I'm not saying anything. I am saying I didn't get on any dinghy boat to do anything. Much less the accusations you have in that photo." He looked down to my hand where I had my phone in my grip. "Whatever it is that woman told you is not true. You can ask Jessica."

"She said Biscuit was out of his special food, and the ferry wasn't running to get you to the mainland." My words drifted off. I jerked up and looked at him. "You don't even live on the island." I gulped.

"Right. And we weren't on the island. I told you I was at home. Trust me. I was having a couple of drinks after what happened at the emergency meeting." He looked at me with his chin pointed down. "I didn't lose as much money as some of the other investors, but it was enough that it punched me in the gut."

"Do you know who else had invested in the development besides you and Raffery?" I asked.

"The Teagardens, who are here, and"—he scratched his head—"I can't think of all of them off the top of my head because it's still so frustrating. I wasn't even going to come here tonight, but I wanted to know what he was thinking and what others were saying."

"Saying about what?" I asked. "The murder?"

"No. The development. I don't know who murdered Leandar, but you and I both know from our work that there's not a short suspect list." He shook his head. "I never even figured I'd be on the list. But if they can find a new development spot, I'd still like to keep my investment."

"That's an option?" I asked.

"Yeah, if your husband agrees to it," he said.

If Patrick agrees to what? I thought, then gave my husband a reasonable doubt. He could have some information he'd not yet told me because I'd been at work all day, as he had, and I changed my plans to come here with Mama, which meant he'd not gotten the opportunity to tell me whatever it was Kirk was talking about.

"If you could talk him into it." He raised his chin. "And your Aunt Maxi. I think our pockets would all benefit from the tourism it would bring." He cleared his throat. "If you'll excuse me, I'm going to go back in and finish my supper before it gets cold. You should too."

"I've lost my appetite," I said and turned to look out over the water.

I laid my forearms on the railing and let my clasped hands dangle over the side while I looked out into the darkness off the side of the boat. There were so many things to think about.

Why on earth would Danielle lie to me? She did look very surprised when I told her Kirk was my ex, but she must have been so far deep into her lie that she couldn't get out of it, so she rolled with it.

"And I thought I was good at reading people." I laughed at myself. "You're getting rusty, kid," I said, knowing I had to do better on my next little visit to see her.

Instead of trying to make sense of it all and just keep to myself what Kirk had told me, even the concerning part Patrick might have a hand in, I ended up going back into the dining room to enjoy eating a meal off those china dishes I was never going to own.

As the evening progressed, the conversation among the guests never seemed to stray toward the topic of the golf course development. Instead, people exchanged pleasantries and shared anecdotes, deliberately steering clear of the elephant in the room. However, the occasional hushed murmur reached my ears, hinting at whispers of Raffery's possible motives for killing Leandar, the real estate agent.

It was like everyone was there to see exactly what Raffery's next move was going to be.

"Leandar had convinced Raffery to sell his farm and hold an estate sale to invest in the Honey Springs Golf Course development," Bev Teagarden told me while we were having an after-dinner cocktail, after the captain had announced that it was last call for the bar and that we were turning the boat around to head back to the Watershed.

In no uncertain way, Bev revealed that with the environmentalist's findings threatening to derail the project, some speculated that Raffery might have sought revenge on the man who had led him down this path.

While I listened to Bev lay out Raffery's motives, I sipped my champagne and observed the beautifully dressed guests laughing and enjoying the cruise on Lake Honey Springs. I couldn't help but feel a sense of unease.

"From what I hear, I think there's a new spot Blackwood Associates is looking at that'll protect at least some of our investments." Bev sipped her drink, her words only leaving me with even more questions for Patrick Cane when I got home. "Especially Caspian Blackwood."

"Why so?" I wondered why she'd say that.

"Caspian has invested all his money into the development. He was going to take early retirement, and now all his money is gone unless he finds another property." She pointed toward the windows looking into the dining room where Raffery had Mama's attention.

Chills crawled up my spine as I looked out at the lake's shimmering surface reflecting the dazzling lights of the cruise vessel. Beneath that serene facade, dark secrets churned, waiting to be revealed.

CHAPTER TEN

"I felt like a fool standing there accusing Kirk of killing Leandar when he was holding the knowledge that Blackwood Associates had already been looking for a new area to develop here," I mumbled through a mouthful of toothpaste.

"I called you a few times today and you were busy, so I didn't get the opportunity to tell you. I wasn't going to tell you on the fly because it's a big investment." Patrick walked over and stood behind me.

He put his large hands on my shoulders and looked at my reflection in the mirror above the single sink. His big brown eyes softened as his mouth curled into a tender smile. His salt-and-pepper hair was cut shorter, what I liked to call his late-spring-to-summer much cooler haircut.

"I would never make any decision without you, especially when it comes to..." I turned around to look him dead in the eyes. I knew what he was going to say, even though I'd yet to hear it from his lips.

"Aunt Maxi's house," we said in unison. I gulped while he gave me a few empathy blinks, his chiseled jaw set.

"If you aren't going to let us move into it, then we need to do something with it." Patrick and I loved Aunt Maxi's house.

It wasn't the house she was living in. It was the property overlooking Lake Honey Springs that had the best views of any place on the lake and where she lived when I was growing up.

The house. The house that was the center of why Patrick and I had broken up before I went off to college.

Making the excuse that I'd gone to college and he was doing his thing made it easy for me to cut off the already long-distance relationship and summer flings.

During the worst time in my life, Aunt Maxi had been going through some financial difficulties. Tourism had all but stopped. The entire town needed a complete makeover, which wouldn't happen for years, and she simply couldn't afford to keep the big house.

She lived alone and found it much easier for her to sell and downsize. One problem, she sold it to Patrick's father, and honestly I thought they'd taken her for a ride. I'd held a grudge for years because I truly thought it was because they'd stolen her dream house, not that she'd sold it. She'd not told me that little bit of information. It was Patrick who did after I'd moved back to Honey Springs.

He still owned the house and was even living there. When we got married, I couldn't bring myself to live in his house, and that's why we'd decided to stay in my cabin. My sweet little cabin. I sighed, looking back over his shoulder.

"Your mom called me and asked to meet with me at the house. I asked if it was about you, and she said, 'In a roundabout way,' but wouldn't tell me. I freaked out and met her there only to find her with Caspian Blackwood, walking our property." Patrick picked up his toothbrush after I stepped out of the way so he could finish getting ready for bed.

"Mom didn't mention a word." I shook my head and picked up the hairbrush to run it through my curly black hair. I stared at myself in the mirror when Patrick bent down to spit in the sink, and my blue eyes looked so tired.

Dull.

"She said she didn't want to even bring it up unless you were willing to part with it because it's a source of pain for you and her too." Patrick pointed out the knockdown drag-out fights my mom and I would have on the phone when I was staying there all those summers and she would make me come home early.

She thought it was because Aunt Maxi wanted me to stay, when Aunt Maxi never had a hand in the decision. Of course, I loved her and wanted to spend all the time I could with her, but it was my love for Patrick that kept me there summer after summer.

"What did you tell Mom and Caspian?" I asked as I left our bathroom, grabbing my robe on the way out.

"I told her I had to talk to you." He followed me out. He'd already had his robe on, and we walked down the steps to finish off our nightly ritual of letting the dogs out one last time, making the coffee so the timer could go off at four a.m., and putting out a fresh outfit in the laundry room so I could get ready in the morning.

Sassy and Pepper's nails danced on the old hardwood floors as they both anticipated going potty for the last time tonight.

Patrick and I sat down in the rocking chairs while the dogs ran off the porch. I wasn't sure if it was the actual nip in the late-spring air, the idea of me losing Aunt Maxi's house due to a big development, or knowing Leandar's killer was still on the loose that gave me a deep chill.

"Can you hand me the blanket?" I asked Patrick since the blanket was draped over the rocking chair he was sitting in.

"What are your thoughts, honey?" He stood up and took the blanket, laid it on my lap, and pushed the edges up around my legs.

"Are you tucking me in?" I teased. "Or buttering me up to agree to the development?"

"I only have your best interest at heart. I'm not tied to the house like you are. When we offered it to Aunt Maxi for supercheap a couple of years ago, she didn't even want it back."

Patrick was right.

Aunt Maxi had long since moved on and even gone on to acquire a lot more houses that she rented out for extra income and to add the boardwalk to her financial portfolio with ownership of a few buildings there. The Bean Hive being one of them.

"What did Caspian propose?" I asked.

"He said the other landowners had agreed to sell their property. Not only is his company paying top dollar, the landowners and any inherited family members will have lifetime membership to the country club," Patrick said. "It also includes all activities. Plus a pool."

"You aren't a golfer," I said.

"I might learn. It could be good for business." He shrugged. "Don't businesspeople like to golf?"

"I don't know. I don't. And you don't even like a pool." I pointed out the fact I could barely get him to the lake to dip his toes in, much less get his entire body in a pool of clean water.

"He mentioned something about holiday parties and even the breakfast with Santa event." Patrick was using my favorite time of the year against me.

"You dirty dog," I teased and leaned over his way to catch a kiss.

I pulled away and saw there was an inherent strength on his face. It was the look he always wore when he had a decision to make and knew it was the right decision but wasn't willing to do anything unless it was good for me.

It was the exact same look when I suggested we dress up for Halloween as a bride and groom and really get married in the hospitality room of the Cocoon Inn. The same look when I wouldn't budge on moving. The same look when the cabin caught fire and we had to rebuild, and when I had the harebrained idea of buying the building next to the Bean Hive and making a roastery.

That was our only investment property besides Aunt Maxi's old house.

"They got a twenty-seven-hole golf course planned that'll appeal to all skill levels. They will have an indoor 4k ultra-HD gold simulator that'll allow golfers to play nine or eighteen holes of some of the most famous golf courses around the world with a virtual driving range,"

Patrick said as he slowly rocked back and forth. "That will allow people to host golf parties indoors. They will offer golf lessons and leagues for all ages."

"It sounds like they got the whole golf thing down pat." I could admit it did sound good.

"There's an event center," he whispered. "Before you jump all over how Babette Cliff will go out of business, Caspian has already talked to her about having two event centers."

"My goodness, he's got it all covered." I wanted to be disappointed in the big development, but I knew it was growth, and we needed to continue to drive tourism to Honey Springs, or we could find ourselves in Aunt Maxi's shoes from years ago.

"Babette is on board. It's going to bring a lot of jobs to Honey Springs. Some of our citizens will get those jobs and not have to drive a few hours to the city to work." Patrick was born and bred in Honey Springs.

His entire heart and mind were invested in the town.

"Is it really the right time to do anything with Blackwood Associates?" I asked Patrick. "I mean, Caspian does have a very good motive to have killed Leandar, and the last thing we need to do is get in bed with him on a bad investment right before he goes to prison."

"I get it." He planted his hands on the arms of the rocking chair and pushed himself up to stand. The dogs were ready to go inside. "Take time and think about it. We have time. Caspian has left town, and he said he'd be back in a week. He would like to meet with you and me."

He stood over me and bent down, giving me a kiss on the top of my head.

"Are you going to bed?" he asked. The moon hung over his right shoulder, and the silhouette of the woods to the side of the house filled the landscape.

"I think I'll stay up and read for a while." It sounded good, and I was going to do that until after Patrick had gone inside with the dogs and left me out there drowning in my own thoughts.

Caspian Blackwood had left town? Did Spencer Shepard let him leave town? Had he already excused Caspian as a suspect?

Instead of wasting my time sitting outside wondering about Caspian, I knew I could run by the sheriff's office in the morning to ask Gloria Dei what she knew.

She always gave in to a good scone temptation.

CHAPTER ELEVEN

There were so many questions I had when I finally fell asleep after Patrick told me about Caspian coming to him to see if he'd be interested in selling Aunt Maxi's old house. The fact Caspian had left town gnawed at me. I didn't even get an ounce of shut-eye.

Or at least, it didn't seem like it when the four a.m. alarm went off.

My bike was still at the boardwalk and the dinghy boat was still on the beach across the road from my cabin, leaving me and Pepper to take the car.

Pepper was extra excited to be going to the coffee shop with me. The temperatures were warm that morning, and even though it was dark, Pepper still wanted to stick his head out the window.

Instead of getting lost in my head, I flipped the radio on so I could at least get into the mindset of getting the coffee shop ready to open, then I'd let myself go over all of my theories.

It sounded good, but my plans changed.

Bunny and Aunt Maxi had beaten me to the coffee shop. They were already sitting down with the whiteboard at one of the café tables, going over the clues, when Pepper and I walked in.

"We've already let the puppy out." Bunny didn't even look up from the whiteboard. She had the puppy resting in her lap and the dry-erase marker in her hand. "And we got all the donuts, quiche, breakfast pies, and coffee started."

"And the coffee station and tea station all ready," Aunt Maxi followed up and gave Pepper the treat on the table she'd apparently anticipated giving him before we'd gotten there. "I missed you yesterday," she said then talked baby talk to him. His little tail wiggled and wagged.

"How was the dinner cruise?" Aunt Maxi asked before I could even hang my bag up on the coatrack.

"You won't believe what we ate off." I took the Bean Hive apron and tied it loosely around my neck and waist. "The bone china."

"Well, I reckon they needed to get some good use out of it." Aunt Maxi cackled.

I quickly checked the industrial coffeepots I needed to take down to Cocoon Inn for their hospitality suite. They were brewing, and soon I'd need to walk them down there unless I could get one of the two sleuths to do it.

"What are you two conjuring up?" I asked and poured some kibble into Pepper's bowl and the puppy's.

The puppy was eager to follow Pepper around and happily started to eat the puppy kibble after seeing his bowl next to Pepper's.

"We are trying to figure out what on earth is going on around here. Or did you forget there was a murder?" Aunt Maxi asked.

"Did you find anything out last night?" Bunny followed her, neither one giving me the opportunity to talk before they darted questions at me.

"Did you know Blackwood Associates is looking at the house and the lakefront property to move the development to your old house?" I poured myself a cup of coffee, taking the opportunity to enjoy it while the puppy was eating.

Pepper would be fine to relax for a bit after he ate. The puppy was a different story. He had to go outside to pee every time he ate.

"And the owner, Caspian, has left town?" I asked and looked over the board. They'd not written anything else down. It looked the same as yesterday.

"Does that mean he's not a suspect?" Bunny asked, peering over her reading glasses perched on the tip of her nose.

"I don't know, but I plan on stopping by to see Gloria Dei at some point today," I told them.

"Then I better go get the apple hand pies in the oven." Bunny groaned as she got up from the table. "She's a sucker for one or two of your hand pies, but apple is her favorite. Luckily, I saw some in the freezer."

Bunny waddled across the floor, her thick black-soled comfort shoes creaking underneath her.

"Did you know?" I asked Aunt Maxi because she seemed so quiet.

"I heard some rumblings about it, and I called your mama because I knew she was going to try to get some business after Leandar died." I detected a hint of censure in her tone.

"Spill it," I told her with easy defiance.

"When I was at the emergency meeting, before you got there," she said, laying out the timeline, "I was talking to Vicky Delaney. She was telling me how she was shelving some reference books by the conference room at the library while she was working, and the Realtor Association was having a meeting. Vicky told me she heard Ursula Scott and Penny talking about Ursula calling Leandar's secretary to see what he had on the books."

"No wonder Mama has a vested interest in the property. I bet she went to all of the listings over there, which are selling for a pretty penny, and all Caspian had to do was give them a few thousand more than their asking price in order for him to buy up all the houses." I lifted the cup of coffee to my lips.

"But there's one holdout." Aunt Maxi grinned. "Patrick Cane. And that house has the best view of all the properties, including the initial development property on Lake Honey Springs."

"But why did Spencer allow Caspian to leave town?" I took the dry-erase marker Bunny had set on the table when she'd gotten up and wrote little bullet points under his name.

"It would make sense he wasn't a suspect, but with all the evidence of how deep he and Leandar were with the development, I could only imagine how much Caspian has lost. Think of the cost of all the work he's already put into it." Aunt Maxi was talking about money.

I wrote down "greed" and "money" under his name.

"Not only that, but his reputation," Aunt Maxi pointed out. "He's a man with a big ego."

"Ego." I wrote it down too.

"I also heard Caspian put all of his retirement money into this development because he had planned to move to Honey Springs and fully retire, but if the gig went south, then he had no money to retire. It would make sense for him to try to salvage something by moving the development to a piece of property that has already gone through all the environmental testing." As I rambled on and on, the thoughts in my head spilled out as to why Caspian should still be a suspect.

"If he did do it, don't you think he'd not try to move the development?" Aunt Maxi had suggested Caspian would try to get out of town as fast as he could, which he had.

"Or do the complete opposite because he thinks he's untouchable." My eyes gazed at the clock behind the counter. It was already five o'clock, and the puppy needed to go potty. "I'll be back. I have to take the coffee down to Cocoon Inn and let the puppy go potty."

"No. No," Aunt Maxi insisted and jumped to her feet. "I'll take the coffee and let the puppy out. In fact, I'll just take the puppy with me today. I have some errands to run, and then I'll stop by Central Park to let him get some exercise."

She walked over to the coat-tree.

"Can I use one of Pepper's leash?" she asked and pointed to the several on the hooks of the coat-tree.

"Of course you can." I smiled even though she was already halfway to the door with one of them clipped on the puppy.

"I'd say 'bye' to Pepper, but he's already asleep." She snickered, nodding to Pepper's bed where he was rolled over on his back with his round and full belly pointing up at the ceiling.

"You try to find out what all you can about Caspian Blackwood and Blackwood Associates." She gave me a task. "Since we did all the prep work to open this morning. You're our only shot at getting this whole thing figured out."

"Do you want Patrick and me to sell the house?" I asked her, stopping her in her tracks.

She bent down and picked up the puppy before she turned.

She stared me straight in the eye. "Roxy Bloom," she said, poking her heart. "This is where our memories lie. Not in any structure made of bricks and sticks. Right here is where I remember our summers together. If it weren't for right here"—she jabbed herself one last time before she gestured her little finger around the coffee shop—"this here wouldn't be, and you wouldn't either. And for that, I'd never go back. Sell the house."

It was her way of telling me how losing her dream house actually made her dreams and mine come true. Her dream of me living in Honey Springs as well as my dream of owning a coffee shop—and what I'd thought was a lost dream, being married to Patrick Cane.

While I went back to refill my mug, I quickly sent Patrick a text to let him know I'd like to talk to Caspian Blackwood myself. Just me and Caspian. In the end, I would give up the house, but this was my chance to physically lay eyes on and talk to the man who had a great deal of motive to kill Leandar.

On my way back to the whiteboard, I remembered all the information Kirk had told me about Danielle. It had not been lost on me. She was more of a suspect than ever, and the fact that she lied to me had lit a fire that put her on my list of people to go back and question.

As I sat at the window bar, my eyes periodically darted between the screen of my phone and the breathtaking scene unfolding outside the window. Lake Honey Springs had slowly started to come to life as the first light of dawn crept over the horizon, casting a myriad of colors across the sky. The sun began its ascent, painting the world in shades of pink, orange, and gold, its rays reflecting off the glassy surface of the lake and creating a shimmering kaleidoscope of light.

There were a few customers who came through the door. Bunny was able to handle them while I continued to search the internet on my phone for anything and everything I could find on Caspian Blackwood's personal and professional life.

The stillness of the early morning was gradually replaced by the soft sounds of the world awakening. The gentle lapping of waves against the shore mingled with the distant calls of birds as they began their morning serenade. The rustle of leaves and the murmur of the wind whispered through the trees, adding to the serene soundtrack of the awakening day.

Inside the coffee shop, the comforting aroma of freshly brewed coffee filled the air, and the gentle hum of the espresso machine provided a soothing backdrop to the peaceful ambiance. Bunny's shoes creaked as she moved behind the counter, the faint clinking of cups and saucers punctuating the quiet atmosphere.

As I continued to scroll through my phone, I delved deeper into the history of Caspian Blackwood and his company, Blackwood Associates. My fingers flew across the screen, uncovering articles and testimonials that painted a picture of a powerful, influential figure whose business dealings were not without controversy.

Caspian's personal life was as carefully curated as his professional one. He was married to a beautiful and equally ambitious woman, and together they had formed a powerful partnership. Their opulent home was a testament to their success, filled with exquisite art, luxurious furnishings, and all the trappings of wealth from what I read in a *Forbes* magazine clip where they'd been featured.

Caspian Blackwood's success as a land developer was partly due to his ability to operate in the gray areas of the law and exploit loopholes to his advantage. While not all his deals were inherently illegal, some of them were ethically questionable and skirted the boundaries of what was considered acceptable.

I continued to look out the window at Lake Honey Springs, and despite the beauty of the sunrise and the serenity of my surroundings, I felt a growing unease as I read about Blackwood's history.

Questions swirled through my mind, and I began to wonder about the true intentions behind the development of the country club and the potential impact it could have on the picturesque landscape I loved so much.

Wetlands rezoning was one of Caspian's most notorious deals that involved the rezoning of a protected wetland area.

Through his connections with local officials, he managed to have the area's environmental status reclassified, allowing him to drain the wetlands and build a luxury housing development on the land. This had severe consequences for the local ecosystem, resulting in the displacement of countless plant and animal species. Was this as illegal as it was immoral?

For each search that proved to be another strike against Blackwood Associates, there were double examples of the good the company was doing by giving back to environmental groups and even various charities.

Another controversial deal I considered shady had to do with gentrification and displacement of residents of a low-income housing complex with the intention of converting it into high-end condominiums. While the project was financially successful, it led to the displacement of hundreds of longtime residents who could no longer afford to live in their own community. Caspian had little regard for the social consequences of his actions, focusing solely on the profits to be made. Watching the video archives of the local news where this took place nearly broke my heart over the homelessness it'd caused.

But the bribery and corruption charges against Blackwood Associates had never stuck, even though Caspian was known to engage in bribery and corruption to secure deals and fast-track approvals for his projects.

There were even charges brought on the company that it claimed and accounted for lavish gifts and under-the-table payments to officials and regulators, ensuring that his projects would receive favorable treatment and bypass environmental and zoning regulations that were dropped.

"What's this?" I couldn't help but take an interest in another claim called "land grabbing" in which Caspian had been accused of acquiring land through underhanded means.

In one instance, he took advantage of a legal loophole to obtain the land rights to a small family farm that had been passed down for generations. The family was forced to leave their ancestral home, while Caspian turned the land into yet another lucrative development.

Immediately, my mind went to Raffery Featherstone.

Had there been an agreement between Raffery and Caspian? More than just Raffery selling farmland in order to invest?

The coffee shop traffic was starting to pick up, and I had to jot down all the things I'd discovered on the internet in just the short amount of time I'd sat there. Bullet point by bullet point, I listed everything I'd learned.

I took one more sip to wash away the thoughts and looked back out the window.

The sun was high in the sky, casting its warm glow on the lake. I resolved to delve further into this mystery and uncover the truth about Caspian Blackwood and his company.

The peaceful sunrise over Lake Honey Springs served as a reminder of the natural beauty that was at stake, and I knew that I couldn't stand idly by while it was threatened.

CHAPTER TWELVE

There'd been a lull between the breakfast rush and the lunch crowd, leaving me some time to take Pepper for a walk and make a phone call to Jessica. Not that I didn't trust Kirk, but Jessica would have no reason to lie.

"Do you mind watching the shop while I take Pepper for a walk?" I asked Bunny, even though I knew she wouldn't mind. "And when I get back, I want to hear all about your anniversary celebration."

She blushed. It was so cute.

As I strolled along the sun-soaked boardwalk, the vibrant midday bustle of people, laughter, and music filled the air. Boaters cruised by on the glistening lake, their laughter and cheerful conversations mingling with the distant hum of outboard motors and happy boating tunes. The weather was absolutely perfect, with a gentle breeze and a clear blue sky that seemed to stretch on forever.

Pepper trotted happily by my side, his eyes gleaming with excitement as he sniffed the myriad of scents wafting on the breeze. I held my phone to my ear, chatting with Jessica about the recent happenings at the Be Happy Spa.

"So, you're saying you haven't had any dealings with Danielle at the spa?" I asked, seeking clarification. I'd told her everything Danielle had told me.

Even the story about how Danielle had run into Jessica.

"That's right, Roxy," Jessica replied. "I didn't run into her on the beach either. But we did have a brief conversation on the ferry ride over about a week ago. Nothing substantial, though."

"Nothing substantial" from Jessica was a loaded statement. Jessica was too nice. She didn't realize just how much she told about herself when talking to people.

As we talked, I couldn't help but feel a sense of relief that Jessica and Kirk weren't involved in whatever was going on with Danielle.

"Plus, we've never stayed overnight here. And Biscuit hasn't either." She only confirmed that Danielle had made it all up.

"Was Biscuit with you when you were on the ferry?" I asked.

"Yes, and you know, now that I think about it…" There was a pause on Jessica's end. "She did ask me about Biscuit's food because she was thinking about getting a puppy."

That part was true. I remembered Shelley and Shanda telling me how Danielle had come in there, mentioning she'd wanted to adopt the puppy she'd named Jessie.

Was Jessie short for Jessica? Had Danielle really put that much thought into it?

The boardwalk was alive with activity, and the energy of the crowd was almost palpable. Kids darted around, laughing and playing, while couples strolled hand in hand, enjoying the beautiful day.

I glanced down at Pepper, who was wagging his tail, clearly enjoying our leisurely walk.

"Oh, Roxy, I actually I need to go," Jessica interrupted. "The man is here about the raccoons at the spa. You know, raccoons have been getting into our trash, and Crissy isn't happy about having to pick it all up. I need to handle this situation."

"Of course, no problem," I said. "Good luck with the raccoon situation. I'll talk to you later."

We said our goodbyes, and I ended the call. As I looked up from my phone, I suddenly smacked right into a solid figure. I stumbled back, my heart racing, and found myself face-to-face with Raffery Featherstone.

"Raffery!" I exclaimed, my mind racing back to the red paint I'd found on the edge of the dinghy. Could he be the one who took the boat? Was he involved in something far more sinister?

His eyes met mine, and I couldn't help but search for answers in his expression. Little did I know, the encounter would be the beginning of a series of events that would lead to the unraveling of a mystery that went far deeper than I could have ever imagined.

"Thank you so much for last night. The dinner cruise was delicious, but those dishes." I gushed. "I have to admit, I was going to try to get those from the estate sale."

"That," he scoffed. We were standing in front of Wild and Whimsy Antiques, where he looked as if he was about to go in. "I really wish there'd been something to celebrate."

"Your son is home." I smiled, knowing everyone loved to talk about their kids.

"Yes. We are happy he is home, but it doesn't help us leave him a legacy, which is what my wife and I had planned on doing with the investment in the country-club development." He frowned.

The more he talked, the more he showed an even bigger motive to have killed Leandar.

"Speaking of your son, he told me about how you love to jug fish." "Love" might've been stretching it, but it gave me a way to bring up the night of Leandar's murder—or morning, however one chose to see it.

"I do. I love everything about Lake Honey Springs. So much so that I wanted to share it with the world." He was still talking about the development.

"Yeah. The night of Leandar's murder, I understand you were jug fishing," I said.

"I told you, I love it, and it relaxes me. It was after the meeting where the mayor dropped the bomb." Raffery's demeanor changed as did the tone of his voice.

It was more stiff, hard.

"Surely you knew the development was going south. Didn't Caspian tell you, as an investor, what was going on?" I asked.

"Are you kidding me?" His brows shot up. "All he would say was how everything was going to work out. I should've known when he got Leandar involved that the deal would go sideways."

"Why do you say that?" I wondered.

"Look around, Roxy." He flung his hands out. "Do you see any other land development happening in Honey Springs? We have all this lakefront property. Leandar has never—" He stopped talking and then corrected himself. "Had never gotten any deal inked. He was a good talker and could probably talk you into turning your coffee shop into some nightclub in ten minutes if he got in front of you."

"I never had to deal with him. I guess since my Aunt Maxi owns the coffee shop and my mom is now a Realtor." I was responding to the thoughts in my head out loud.

"I was hoping when your mom took over the real estate office downtown after…" He shook his head. "You know what happened, so I don't need to bring that up, but the facts are the facts. Leandar made too many mistakes and talked a good talk that he couldn't walk, which ultimately got him killed."

"Yes. He did. Back to your jug fishing." I stopped him when I saw him take a step toward the door of Wild and Whimsy. "Did you happen to use Andrew Noro's dinghy boat?"

"Why would I do that?" He snarled like it was the silliest thing in the world.

"Because it has some red paint on the edges." I gulped, not really sure if it was red paint or blood. "I saw it the other day when I used it. And Danielle mentioned it."

"Mentioned what?" He interrupted me and jerked upright, standing over me.

"She said someone had used it the night Leandar was killed, and I wondered if you might've broken down. You borrowed it." I could feel the tension coming off him as I walked the fine line between us.

"What are you saying, Roxanne?" It was never good when someone used my full name, especially when that someone was twice my size and towered over me. "Are you accusing me of killing Leandar?"

"I'm not doing anything. I'm trying to find out who was on the lake the night he was murdered, and if anyone who might've been out there saw something." I tried not to swallow or shift my eyes away from him.

"There you are!" Bev Teagarden must've seen us from inside the antique shop because she swung the door open and greeted us. "Is everything okay?" She found herself outside standing next to me and Raffery, still in our stare down.

"We are fine and finished," Raffery said in a deep Southern tone. "It was good to see you, Roxy. Tell your mama and them I said hello."

And with one hard nod, he not only walked away but also didn't answer my question.

Bev fidgeted. "Is everything okay?" she leaned in and whispered once Raffery had gone into her shop.

"It's fine. I was asking Raffery about the development. That's all." I offered her a smile to help her relax.

"Good. Isn't it a shame?" She shook her head. "But we are hoping you do want to sell Maxine's old house. It'll be so good for Honey Springs to have something new to bring in more tourism. As it is, I'm going to have to pay a small fortune for the Featherstones' bone china I was hoping to score at the auction."

"I wanted those too." My voice ticked up. "That's why he's here?" I avoided the topic of Aunt Maxi's old house.

I wasn't going to make any decisions about that property until I got in front of Caspian Blackwood.

"Yes." Bev held up both hands with her fingers crossed. "Wish me luck I can get him down to a reasonable price."

"Good luck," I told her as she turned and hurried back inside the shop. "Why is he selling the bone china if he's not moving?" I asked myself and decided to worry about that at a later time.

I had to get to the dinghy boat and run it back across the water so I could question Danielle about all of her lies.

Luckily, the day was nice, and a brisk walk would do me good if I'd not been too preoccupied by the conversation I'd had with Raffery on the boardwalk. It wasn't so much the conversation but the change in his body language that threw me off. And the fact that he needed to sell the family china now that he wasn't moving into the development seemed a little odd to me too.

Pepper was really good at being off the leash, so he ran around and sniffed the area, staying close to me.

The dinghy was exactly where I'd left it. And in the daylight, I could clearly see it wasn't paint. It was a bloody handprint.

My jaw tensed. My heart beat, and I knew what I had to do.

"Spencer, I think you need to come to the crime scene," I told him when he answered the phone. "I've got a dinghy boat here, and it sure does look like it has a bloody handprint on it."

Spencer babbled a few things about why I was at the crime scene when it was still considered a crime scene, but instead of wanting to hear about it, he then told me to forget it, and he'd be there in a minute because he was downtown, which really was about five minutes away.

The sound of hard footsteps, crunching leaves, and snapping branches were heard before I saw him, but from the time between each step, I knew it was him rushing to the beach area.

"Do I even want to know how you know this is here?" he asked, bending down to look at the print.

Pepper was excited to see Spencer. Spencer bent down to pet Pepper. Pepper sat like a good boy, and I took the opportunity to clip his leash on him.

"I'm going to tell you anyways because I think Danielle Quillen is the killer." The words fell out of my mouth as he slowly twisted his neck and looked up at me from underneath his sheriff's hat.

"I'm listening." He dragged his bag closer to the dinghy and opened it. He put gloves on his hands. He took out all sorts of baggies for the samples he was taking from the bloody handprint.

I told him how I'd gone to see Danielle and how odd it was that she'd not come into the Bean Hive the day after Leandar's murder.

"She came in every morning before that, so it was odd. You know, noticeable." I shrugged. "The day Leandar was murdered"—I prepared myself for the repercussions I was about to get because Spencer wasn't going to like that I'd kept this from him—"Leandar came into the coffee shop when he saw her sitting through the window while he passed by on the boardwalk."

"I'm listening." Spencer must've known there was a doozy coming his way. He stood up and used the tip of his forefinger to tip the hat up enough just so he could have a clear view of my face.

"He threatened to expose her if she didn't keep her mouth shut, and he was talking about the development." I tugged my lips together.

"And you felt like this was something you didn't need to tell me. I mean, there was a threat to expose something she'd done, making it a clear motive for her not to want that secret out, which would make her the number one suspect, not Caspian Blackwood." His jaw tensed, and he stared at me as if he wanted some sort of explanation.

I gave in to the awkward pause I tried so desperately not to fall for.

"You told me to keep my ears open, and I went to see her because I knew of the exchange and..." I gulped, showing my fear.

"You knew it was a bad idea. And you still did it." He shook his head. "Keeping your ears open is just that. You're good at gossip. That's why people love going to the Bean Hive. I didn't ask you to put yourself in front of a killer."

My head was stuck on me being good at gossip. Clearly, he didn't know me, and I never gossiped. Yes, there was a lot of hearsay and ho-hums going on at the coffee shop, and I admit I was listening, but I never said an ill word or lie or even participated in those conversations.

Now, if it was my immediate family, I might've opened my mouth a time or two, but never to the customers.

"You listen for any clues, like someone who is being threatened by the victim, and you call me." He was laying out the way things were supposed to go like I was an idiot or something. "Then we go and talk to the person who was threatened by the now-dead victim and had a motive."

There were a few minutes of him cursing under his breath, looking at the boat, cursing some more, bending down, and looking across the lake before he stood up, and then he glared at me.

"I'm sorry. I know you don't gossip, but this case…" He shook his head with a look of disgust on his face. "The mayor is on me about it. This was a very serious deal with a lot of investors who are going to lose a lot of money."

"There's hope they won't." I hated to mention it to him, but I could clearly see this was also on his personal radar as much as it was mine. "I have a meeting that's being set up with Caspian Blackwood to talk about selling him Aunt Maxi's old house. The land around it is filled with houses that owners are happy to sell and that has already been developed."

The land had already gone through the entire process of being surveyed by environmentalists and all that. Like I'd said, it was the best view of Lake Honey Springs.

"I know that's going to be hard for you." Spencer showed his soft side. "But it still doesn't help matters that you have been sitting on this evidence. Do I even want to know how long this boat has been sitting here? In the elements?"

"Probably not. I thought it was paint until I came back to drive it back over to the cabin Danielle is renting." I glanced across the lake where you could see the little cabin.

"Paint?" Spencer closed his eyes and clenched his jaw as if he were preparing himself to hear what I was talking about.

"Yeah. I was on the Featherstone dinner cruise the other night and Caldwell, his son…" I told him the story.

"I know Caldwell." He rolled his wrist as if to tell me to hurry along and finish the story.

"He and I were talking about jug fishing, and he mentioned how his dad loved to jug fish and told me that Raffery had just gone out the night before."

"As in the night, or morning hours, that Leandar was murdered?" Spencer asked for clarity.

"Yes. Then I thought what if this was paint, which it's clearly not." I knew it now. "Because Caldwell told me how Raffery used red paint on his jugs."

There was no need to explain to Spencer about why Raffery would paint the jugs because everyone around here already was very familiar with jug fishing.

"Raffery will be so mad if he hears you think he killed Leandar." Spencer should've told me this a few minutes ago. His jaw dropped open. "Geez, Roxy, don't tell me you confronted Raffery Featherstone."

"Okay." I shrugged and caught sight of a boat moving down the lake, going toward the beach in front of the cabin Danielle had rented. "I won't tell you."

"If you mess up this case," he started to say then turned when the boat motor got louder as it approached. "What on earth is going on?"

"That's Danielle with her stuff." I pointed my chin when I noticed Danielle, her hands full of bags and a suitcase, walking to the dock where the dinghy had been tied up. "She's leaving town."

"Who is driving the speedboat?" Spencer asked and frantically looked at the evidence he'd just collected. "This is going to have to be enough."

Quickly he gathered all the tubes, baggies, and whatever else he'd collected and threw it in his duffel, zipping it closed and tossing it in the dinghy.

"What are you doing?" I asked.

"You got photos of this, right?" He rolled up the rope that was tied to the front of the small boat, though I'd not had to tie it to anything because I'd dragged it up on the beach.

There was only one reason to toss the loose rope inside. To drive it.

"Yes, but are you going to go over there?" I asked as if Spencer standing in it didn't give me the clue.

"I'm going to go stop her from leaving." He sat down on the small bench.

When he turned back to pull the engine to life, I grabbed Pepper and hopped in.

"Get out!" he yelled over the hum of the motor. "Get out! This is official business."

I sat down next to him on the small bench and crossed my arms.

"I'm not moving. I need answers from her, too, as her lawyer." I knew that was really going to throw him for a zinger.

"Her what?" he screamed with fury in his eyes. "Please don't tell me you offered services to her."

Pepper hung over the side with his ears flapping in the wind, not a care in the world.

I stared straight ahead, not saying a word. In reality, she'd not become a client, but now I wanted answers. She'd not only dragged the entire town into this mess but also brought Kirk into it. Even though sending him to jail for a murder would be satisfying, making him the scapegoat certainly was not.

CHAPTER THIRTEEN

My heart pounded in my chest as the dinghy bounced across the water, its outboard motor roaring with determination. Sheriff Spencer Shepard gripped the handle, his jaw set and eyes focused on the speedboat ahead of us. Danielle, now the number one suspect in Leandar's murder, was making a desperate attempt to flee town with all her luggage.

"Can't this thing go any faster?" I shouted over the wind and the noise of the motor.

Spencer shook his head, his expression grim. "We're pushing it to the limit, Roxy! Just hold on!"

The wind whipped through my hair as we raced after Danielle's speedboat, which was slicing through the water like a hot knife through butter. She was supposed to be in town, cooperating with the investigation, but her sudden flight was a blatant admission of guilt.

As the distance between us and Danielle's speedboat began to shrink, I couldn't help but think back to all the signs we'd missed. The way she'd shifted the blame and motives onto others, skillfully manipulating us to focus on anyone but her. But now, her true colors were showing.

My knuckles turned white as I gripped the side of the dinghy, my gaze locked on the fleeing speedboat. The adrenaline coursed through my veins, fueling my determination to catch Danielle and bring her to justice.

"Roxy, I need you to call for backup," Spencer shouted over the roar of the engines. "We can't let her get away!"

I fumbled for my phone, my fingers shaking with nerves and excitement as I dialed the number. "This is Roxy Bloom," I said, struggling to make myself heard over the chaos. "I'm in a dinghy boat with Spencer, and we're in pursuit of Danielle. She's fleeing on a speedboat, and we need immediate backup!"

Big Bib, on the other end of the line, acknowledged my call and promised assistance. I could see Danielle glance back at us, her eyes wide with fear. The sight only fueled my determination to see her captured.

"I called Big Bib!" I screamed through the sounds of the very active chase. "He's going to jump in a boat."

I knew if I called him, he was already on the marina and would stop the speedboat faster than the local coast guards.

Spencer maneuvered the dinghy expertly, taking advantage of every opportunity to close the gap between us and Danielle. The sound of another speedboat approaching filled the air, and I knew it was Big Bib on his way.

"We've got her now," Spencer said, a fierce resolve in his voice. "She's not getting away this time."

As the chase continued, I steeled myself for whatever lay ahead. The stakes were higher than ever, and I was ready to do whatever it took to bring Danielle to justice and ensure that Leandar's murder would not go unpunished.

"What are you doing, man?" The driver of the speed boat Danielle was in had slowed. He was screaming at Big Bib.

Big Bib didn't say a word. His lips were so tight, you couldn't even see them behind his beard. He nodded back to the dinghy boat and pointed.

"Danielle Quillen, I asked you not to leave town when I talked to you the other night. It sure does appear that you're leaving." Spencer flashed his badge to the other boat driver while Big Bib steadied the speedboat, allowing the dinghy to get closer.

"You can't keep me here." Danielle couldn't bring herself to look at Spencer or me.

When the dinghy got next to the boat, Spencer swung his leg over, planting his foot on the edge of the speedboat to keep us joined.

"I'm going to have to take you in for questioning for the murder of Leandar Taylor." Spencer reached around his utility belt and unclipped the handcuffs. "You can either come with me willingly or not."

The cuffs clinked together as he wagged them in the air.

"You didn't say anything about a murder." The boat driver looked shocked. "I have no idea who this woman is. I met her at the bee farm yesterday, and she asked if I could come take her to the mainland to catch her ride to the airport."

The innocent bystander was flabbergasted.

"Thank you. I will need you to write all of your contact information down as well as give me your license. I'll need to snap a photo of it." Spencer pointed to Big Bib's boat when Danielle got up to get on the dinghy. "We are going to have Big Bib take us to the marina."

Big Bib didn't lose his manners. He walked to the edge of his boat closest to where Danielle was standing and offered her a hand.

"If you don't mind, hook up the dinghy to the back. I'm going to need to take it in for evidence even though the bloody handprint is mostly gone from the water and the little stunt you pulled." Spencer made no bones about it. He wasn't letting Danielle off easy.

Big Bib didn't ask any questions. He did what Spencer had asked him to do while Spencer took a photo of the speedboat driver's license and had the man write down his information in Spencer's little notebook he kept in his sheriff's uniform pocket.

"I told you I didn't do it." Danielle directed her statement to me when she crossed over from one boat to the other. "I thought you believed me."

"I did until I talked to Kirk," I said flatly and moved to Big Bib's boat once the dinghy was securely tied up. "I'm guessing you didn't think I talked to my ex."

"I'm sorry. But I didn't do it. I didn't," she insisted. "And I'm going to pay you to be my lawyer."

"I knew I should've pushed you overboard when I had the chance back at the beach," Spencer said. There was no joking tone to his voice. "You might'swell all come down to the station, if that's the case."

"I didn't say I was going to take Danielle on as a client." My brows knotted when I glared at Danielle to see if I could read her body language, not really sure if I could trust her.

"Just talk to me when we get to the station. I'll tell you anything you want to know," she pleaded.

Spencer let the other boater leave and gave Big Bib the signal to go.

"You want to hear what I have to say," Danielle's voice was caught in the wind, barely able for me to hear. "Caspian Blackwood killed Leandar Taylor."

That was clear.

CHAPTER FOURTEEN

"Don't say another word," I told her once we got to the marina. "I'll meet you at the sheriff's department."

Pepper had nestled himself next to her, which told me she couldn't be all that bad. He was a good judge of character, and if he was comfortable with her right now, then I was going to take my sweet pup's lead.

I assured her she would be okay and I'd be right behind them. I only had to jump into my car that was parked in the parking lot of the boardwalk.

Quickly, I took Pepper back to the Bean Hive, and by the time I got there, Bunny Bowowski had already left for the day. Shanda was at the coffee bar when I walked in, and Shelley was with a customer.

"I'd love to watch Pepper. Do you want me to drive him home after I get off?" Shanda asked.

"If you don't mind. I'm not sure how long I'll be." I glanced at the puppy. "Just drop Jessie off too."

I didn't worry about checking in with Shelley because she was upselling the customer on buying a few of this morning's donuts, but I did move around behind the counter to grab some leftovers that were probably not going to sell this late at night.

Donuts and sheriff's department paired really well when I needed to get some answers.

With the donuts and some coffee, I jumped into my car and headed straight to the department, where I found my mama already in the interview room with Danielle.

"It's about time." Mama stood up, her hand firmly planted on Danielle's shoulder. "We've been waiting."

"You couldn't've been waiting too long." I glanced between the two and put the coffee and bag of donuts on top of the table. "What on earth are you doing here?"

"I called her. She's been so helpful with everything, and I trust her." Danielle was seeking comfort from anyone she could get it from. "I know she's your mom, and I sure could use a mom right now."

"That's great, but I'm going to need to talk to my client alone." I gave Danielle a hard look before I shifted it to Mom.

"Fine. But"—Mom lingered before she pulled the bag of donuts to her—"I'll leave you with one of these and go take the rest to butter up the staff." She winked, using the sales tactic she had cultivated to perfection with clients when she was showing their house for sale.

She would come to the Bean Hive and have me give her some fresh donuts that could be heated up in the oven of the house she was selling. She claimed it made the home smell amazing and homey, a big selling point because somehow it played mind games with the potential buyers.

And she let the interested buyers have one of the just-out-of-the-oven donuts. I didn't question her, and she didn't question how I did things, so it was fine.

I walked Mama out of the room and shut the door behind her.

"I'm sorry, Roxy. I am, but I was starting to get nervous when Caspian didn't come back like he said he was going to." Danielle started off the conversation, right off the bat answering the questions I had intended to ask.

"You already know he put all of his retirement into the development, but what you didn't know was the last development he had with

Leandar went south. Like over-one-hundred-thousand-dollars south. Caspian told me if this deal with Leandar didn't make up for the money he'd lost the investors in the last go-round, then Leandar would never make another deal in his life." She cried as she told me the story.

I sat there, listening.

"After you saw Leandar in the Bean Hive threatening me..." She blinked. I could tell what she was about to say might throw me a little, so I sucked in a deep breath to prepare my facial features so they wouldn't appear to be shocked. "I met him later that day, and he tried to pay me off. He told me if I didn't say anything, he'd give me the shares he invested in the development because he said he was afraid for his life."

"I thought you said earlier he had threatened to expose you for some illegal dealings." I didn't go into too much detail. She knew what I was talking about.

"It wasn't really that. I mean, yes, he had some information about what some might consider immoral business decisions, but I can assure you, I've never done anything illegal. Just like the development here." She shook her head. "They could definitely build the country club. There's nothing illegal about doing it, but it would create a terrible situation for the environment of Lake Honey Springs. Illegal?" She continued to shake her head. "No. Immoral? I'd say yes. Not the right thing to do."

"Let me get this straight." I reached across the table and filled up two glasses with the water from the provided pitcher. I picked one up and took a drink before I walked one over to her. "Leandar knew he couldn't really hurt you with the information he deemed illegal, immoral, or whatever. He ended up trying to bribe you because he knew the consequences of his actions would be murder, and from Caspian?"

I continued to walk around the room so I could get some good oxygen to my brain. It always helped me think.

"I believe so," she agreed. "Caspian came to see me after the emergency meeting. He was the one who took the dinghy boat across to the land. It was late, and the ferry had stopped running. He said he would take the dinghy over, and he did. The next morning when I woke up, it was there, but he wasn't. I figured he'd driven it back over and caught the first ferry back."

This was information I could easily get from Big Bib if Caspian did take the ferry.

"Caspian is your alibi, not Jessica and Kirk or even poor Biscuit?" I asked.

She nodded.

"Caspian knew Kirk and Jessica from their investment. I'd never had any dealings with them, so he told me to say I was at the spa if anyone asked where I was. He even gave me the receipts I produced for you." She frowned and picked up the glass of water with a shaky hand.

"What did the two of you talk about when he was at the cabin?" I asked.

"He told me about how Leandar had messed up again. He was a mess. He was drinking and brought the liquor with him. He said Leandar was going to be a dead man, and he couldn't stop it." She closed her eyes. Large tears dropped from them.

There was a box of tissues in the middle of the table along with the water pitcher. I reached across the table and got them for her. She plucked one out when I set the box down.

"He also told me I should get out of town because this was the second time I'd written a report where the development shouldn't've been built. Yesterday, when you came by, I was already planning to leave, but you stayed too long, and I didn't get a chance to get on the ferry. After you left, I took a walk to try and think what to do. I just so happened to find myself at the bee farm where the man with the boat and his family had docked to grab some fresh honey. I asked if I could get a ride from him in the morning, and I paid for their honey." She continued to shake her head and internally beat herself up as she cried.

"Did you hear from Caspian after he took the dinghy from the dock that night after the emergency meeting?" I asked, wondering if he admitted to her how he killed Leandar, and if he did, in fact, commit the murder.

"No. Like I said, he agreed to take the dinghy and bring it back the next day. I went to bed. I saw all the lights over there that morning, and that's when I saw the dinghy boat was back. I just figured Caspian brought the boat back and got a ride." Her timeline was off. "Do you think he used it to meet Leandar at the development and then…" She couldn't bring herself to say it.

"Someone jogging on the beach found Leandar that morning. It's safe to say Leandar had only one reason to be there." It was an assumption, but knowing Leandar, there was really only one thing that would get him out of bed to go to the development, and that was money. "To talk to someone who knew enough about the development to have a new idea of what to do with the news you delivered at the emergency meeting. Someone had to entice him enough to get him there."

It went without saying that Leandar couldn't resist a deal or making a deal happen, especially after a million-dollar deal had recently gone south.

The door of the interrogation room opened, and Spencer walked in with a file. He dropped it on the table and motioned for me to sit next to Danielle. I didn't.

"May I ask your client a few questions?" he asked me as I took a seat across from her.

"Sure." I leaned back into the chair and folded my hands in my lap. "I'll interrupt if I don't think you should answer these questions, Danielle."

My senses heightened and my mind raced like it used to when I would meet clients at a police station when they were about to be charged with something. As her lawyer, it was my job to ensure she was treated fairly, and I was prepared to intervene if necessary. Sheriff Spencer took his place at the end of the table, a stern expression on his face as he flipped through a folder containing information on the case.

"All right, Danielle," he began, his tone firm but not unkind. "I need you to walk me through your evening, starting from when Caspian Blackwood came to your cabin."

Danielle shifted uncomfortably in her seat, her voice shaky as she recounted the events of that night. "Caspian arrived around nine p.m., asking if he could use my dinghy to get back across the lake since he had missed the last ferry. I didn't see any harm in it, so I agreed and helped him get the dinghy ready."

Sheriff Spencer raised an eyebrow, his gaze intense as he pressed on with his questioning. "Did you notice anything unusual about Mr. Blackwood's behavior or appearance?"

Danielle hesitated for a moment before answering. "He seemed a bit anxious, maybe even a little frightened, but I didn't think much of it at the time."

"What happened after Mr. Blackwood left in the dinghy?" Spencer asked, leaning forward slightly.

Danielle swallowed hard, her voice barely above a whisper as she continued her account. "I went back inside the cabin and spent the rest of the evening there. I didn't see or hear anything out of the ordinary until the next morning when I saw all the flashing lights across the lake. The dinghy was back."

"Can you think of anyone who might have had a reason to harm Mr. Blackwood?"

Spencer's question seemed to catch Danielle off guard, and I could see the fear in her eyes as she considered her response.

Before she could answer, I quickly interjected, "My client is not obligated to speculate on the motives of others, Sheriff."

He nodded in acknowledgment, though his gaze remained fixed on Danielle. "Very well. Did you have any prior interactions or conflicts with Mr. Blackwood or his company, Blackwood Associates?"

Danielle nodded her head. "I've worked for him on a few projects."

"Did all of those projects pass your environmental tests?" he asked.

"All but the development here in Honey Springs and another one in Massachusetts." It was the first time I'd heard her name a development in another state that went south.

"Did Mr. Blackwood lose a lot of money because of that deal?" Spencer asked.

"I can't let her answer that. She doesn't know Mr. Blackwood's company's finances. She's subcontracted by him." I interrupted again and gave Spencer a "come on" look.

"Did Mr. Blackwood say anything to you about why he was on this side of the lake or what he had been doing earlier in the evening?" Spencer inquired, his voice tinged with suspicion.

Again, I interrupted before Danielle could respond. "My client has already told you everything she knows about Mr. Blackwood's activities that evening. Continuing down this line of questioning is not productive."

Sheriff Spencer sighed, his frustration evident as he closed the folder and leaned back in his chair. "All right, Roxy, I understand. But we need to get to the bottom of this."

"Then you need to be checking with Caspian Blackwood," I said, because it was apparent Spencer had gotten a lead or some information that made Caspian the reason for him to bring Danielle here.

"Can you please stand up?" he asked Danielle. She looked at me with a bit of confusion.

I nodded. She stood up and so did I.

Spencer walked over to us, standing about four inches taller than Danielle.

"Stand up as tall as you can, please." He was at least respectful of her, and she did everything he told her, even extending her arms out to the side.

He was obviously checking her arm-length span, and I wasn't sure why, but he had to have some reason.

"That's all for now. You can go back home. Just keep your phone on you and answer if I call." He turned and took the file off the table.

"Hold on," I told her and hurried out the door after him, stopping him in the hallway. "Spencer, what was that?"

"I'm letting her go." He shrugged, tucking the file up underneath his armpit.

"What about the blood?" I asked. "On the dinghy?"

"It's not Leandar's blood type. But it could be Caspian's. I've got a call into his lawyer about talking to him. While she has been in there, we had a warrant issued to search the cabin, but the Noros gave us full permission."

No wonder I had so much time with her inside before he came into the room.

"I'm not sure when Caspian will be back in town, but I do know we found blood on the dock where Danielle was staying on the island." Spencer wasn't convinced the killer had taken the dinghy to the development, killed Leandar, and then took the dinghy back.

"You let her go pretty easy." I had to get to the root of why he'd just let Danielle go without even telling her to stay in town.

"Because Kevin gave me his final autopsy, and there's literally zero sand on Leandar except for the backside of his clothes. Not a speck on the bottom of his shoes or even inside his shoes." Spencer and I both knew that no matter how hard you tried or what shoes you had on, the heels of your shoes always kicked up sand into the back of your shoes.

"Wait." My eyes lowered. I slightly turned my head. "Are you saying someone placed Leandar there?"

His silence was all I needed to know the answer.

"There's a murder crime scene somewhere," I said, almost in disbelief.

"And my investigation just got a little more complicated." His jaw tensed. "Danielle couldn't carry Leandar or wasn't tall enough to hit him with the blow to the head that actually killed him."

"That's why you had her stand up," I said, thinking that was a really great observation, something I'd not come up against in my past life as a lawyer.

He continued to stare at me.

"What?" I asked just as my phone rang. "It's Patrick. Hold that thought."

I turned my head slightly to take his call.

"Can I call you back?" I asked him.

"Caspian Blackwood is in town, and we are going to go meet at the house. Can you come?" he asked.

"Caspian is in town?" My head swung back around and looked at Spencer. "And he's at Aunt Maxi's old house right now?"

"Are you sure you're okay?" Patrick asked with a worried tone.

"Yes." Spencer gave me the double-guns gesture with his fingers. "Go talk to him," he mouthed.

"Yes. I'm fine. I'll be there in a few." I hung up the phone with Patrick. "I don't like bringing my husband into this."

"You agreed to snoop around, and his lawyer sure didn't tell me he was in town." Spencer took his keys out of his pocket. "Ready?"

"Ready? You're not going with me." I shook my head. "No. I'm going to go by myself, and after I talk with him about the property, you're more than welcome to swoop in."

"You all good?" Mama had popped her head around the corner at the far end of the hallway.

"We are." I opened the door of the interrogation room and gestured for Danielle to leave. "I'm assuming you've missed your plane home."

I didn't know what time she'd booked a flight, but I did know that it took over two hours to get to either airport she could've flown out of, so that would put her on a late-night flight, if there was one.

"Yeah. I was taking an Uber to the airport, and I guess I can just get another one to spend the night at the airport," Danielle said, and Mama overheard.

"That will not do. You can stay with me. And what about Jessie?" Mama asked about the adoptable puppy at the Bean Hive.

"I do love him," Danielle whined before she smiled. "Do you mind if I stay the night? I'll be out of your hair bright and early."

"You will because you, my dear, are going to show up when Roxy gets to the Bean Hive, get that little Jessie, and then go home to make a good, clean life for yourself." Mama cracked me up sometimes.

I never knew when she was going to say something that made so much sense and other times make not a lick of it. The more I got to know my mom as an adult, the closer we got. Today, we'd just gotten a little closer.

CHAPTER FIFTEEN

Standing in the once-vibrant and bustling house that used to be Aunt Maxi's, I felt a strange mixture of emotions. The large house was filled with memories of my childhood summers spent in Honey Springs, and it was where Patrick and I had first met as teenagers. I took a deep breath, knowing that selling the house was a difficult decision but necessary for the future prosperity of Honey Springs. The development of the country club would bring much-needed tourism and employment opportunities to the area.

Caspian Blackwood, the enigmatic figure behind Blackwood Associates, was there to discuss the deal and finalize the sale. His presence was commanding, and I couldn't help but feel a little intimidated as we shook hands and exchanged pleasantries. As we gathered in the living room, Caspian began to outline the agreement and the perks that would come with it.

"As a token of our appreciation for your cooperation in this project, Roxy and Patrick, you and your family will receive lifetime memberships to the Honey Springs Country Club," he began, a confident smile on his face. "This membership will grant you unlimited access to all the amenities and facilities we have to offer."

He proceeded to list the perks that we would enjoy as members of the country club. "First and foremost, you'll have access to our state-of-the-art golf course, complete with a fully equipped pro shop and a team of professional instructors. Additionally, you'll be able to enjoy our tennis courts, swimming pool, and fitness center, all maintained to the highest standards for your enjoyment."

I listened intently, trying to picture the new country club and the benefits it would bring to Honey Springs. Caspian continued, "Our clubhouse will feature an upscale restaurant and bar, where you can dine on exquisite cuisine prepared by our renowned executive chef. And, of course, the country club will host numerous social events and gatherings throughout the year, providing ample opportunities for networking and entertainment."

As he spoke, I could sense the passion and determination behind his vision for the country club. It was clear that he wanted to create something truly exceptional, and I couldn't help but feel a glimmer of excitement at the prospect of what lay ahead for our small town.

"Lastly," Caspian concluded, "as lifetime members, you and your family will receive priority access to all our facilities, as well as preferential rates for any services or events you wish to host at the club."

With a mixture of sadness and anticipation, Patrick and I signed the papers, sealing the deal and ushering in a new chapter for Honey Springs.

The house that held so many memories would be replaced by a thriving country club, and I could only hope that our decision would ultimately prove to be the right one for the community we loved so dearly.

“How about a toast?” Caspian’s sly smile poked something in my gut when he pulled out the bottle of bubbly and a few glasses. “I always like to seal the deal with a little champagne.”

After a quick toast, Caspian walked over to look out over Lake Honey Springs from the floor-to-ceiling windows.

As Caspian continued to speak about the country club and its potential impact on Honey Springs, I found myself captivated by his charm and charisma. He had a way of making everything he said sound like the most enticing opportunity, and I could feel myself being drawn in by his enthusiasm.

However, as I observed him, my mind started to drift back to the research I had done on Caspian Blackwood and his company, Blackwood Associates, from my laptop at the Bean Hive.

I remembered the numerous shady deals and controversies that seemed to follow him from his previous developments. There were allegations of environmental damage, financial misconduct, and even bribery. Although nothing had ever been definitively proven, the pattern of questionable behavior was impossible to ignore.

I also recalled the information I had uncovered about Caspian's personal financial situation, not to mention what Danielle had said about their past history.

From what I had gathered, he had invested a significant portion of his retirement savings into this Honey Springs project. If the development didn't go through, he stood to lose everything. This knowledge made me question his motivations even further. Was he genuinely passionate about revitalizing Honey Springs, or was he simply desperate to save himself from financial ruin?

As these thoughts swirled through my mind, I found myself looking at Caspian with a newfound sense of caution. I could no longer ignore the nagging feeling that there was more to this man and his intentions than met the eye.

Though Patrick and I had already signed the papers, I knew I couldn't simply sit back and watch the development unfold without doing my due diligence.

I needed to ensure that the future of Honey Springs was in good hands and that the community we cherished wouldn't be irreparably harmed by the development.

I smiled politely at Caspian as he concluded his presentation, all the while mentally preparing myself for the questions I was about to ask him.

I was committed to protecting Honey Springs and its residents, and

I wouldn't rest until I was certain the development of the country club was truly in the best interests of our community.

“Do you have any questions for me?” Caspian opened the door all on his own.

“Yes. Why did you go to the island after the emergency meeting?” I asked.

“Roxanne.” Patrick’s eyes grew big as my name spit out of his mouth.

“Well? It’s a valid question. I’m a lawyer, and I love Honey Springs. I think we deserve to know what he might have to do with Leandar.” I shrugged and took a sip of the champagne.

“I see you have a very active mind.” Caspian grinned. “There’s no big conspiracy. From what I gather, I’m guessing Leandar’s dealings have come back to haunt him. I thought you owned a coffee shop.”

“She does.” Patrick spoke up over me. “But we should go.”

“No.” I shook my head. “I think I will stay and find out some more answers now that we’ve funded his retirement.”

My suspicions growing, I took a deep breath and decided to confront Caspian about the issues that had been gnawing at me. I could sense Patrick's unease as I prepared to ask Caspian some difficult questions, but I couldn't let these concerns go unaddressed.

"Caspian," I began, my voice steady and firm. "I have to ask you about Leandar's murder. It seems that you had a motive, considering the development was on the brink of collapsing and your retirement was at stake. Can you explain your relationship with Leandar and why some people might think you had a reason to want him gone?"

Caspian's confident demeanor faltered for a moment, but he quickly regained his composure. "Leandar and I had our differences, but I would never resort to violence. Business is business, and sometimes things don't go as planned. That doesn't mean I would ever harm someone."

I pressed on, unwilling to let him evade the question. "What about the threats your investors made against Leandar if the deal fell through? I heard from Danielle that you mentioned, in no uncertain terms, that Leandar's days were numbered."

Caspian's face flushed, and he shifted uncomfortably in his seat. "Those were just words, Roxy. I didn't mean anything by it. People say things in the heat of the moment, but it doesn't mean they'll act on it."

Out of the corner of my eye, I could see Patrick fidgeting, clearly anxious about the direction the conversation was taking. But I couldn't stop now. I needed answers.

"What about the scratch on your arm?" I asked, gesturing toward the visible mark. "And the blood we found on the dinghy? How do you explain that?"

Caspian hesitated before responding. "The scratch is from the dingy accident, nothing more." He laughed as if he were having the memory. "I'm not a boater, and I had a few too many drinks at the bar at the Be Happy Spa with one of my investors."

Was he talking about Kirk?

"I knew Danielle had the cabin, so I walked down there and asked her if I could use the dinghy to get across the lake. She didn't mind at all, but I couldn't untie it right. I scratched my arm on the wood post, and the blood dripped down my arm."

He pulled his sleeve up a little to show a full gash that was still looked pretty raw.

"I sat in the boat and was a bit dizzy. I'm sure it was from the booze. I held on to the boat on both sides to steady myself so I wouldn't flip. Eventually, I slipped down into the boat and fell asleep." He didn't even drive the boat. He never left the dock. "I got up sometime during the middle of the night and headed back to the dock at the bee farm where I hitched a ride back with the ferry guy."

I could feel Patrick trying to interrupt, but I ignored him, my focus solely on Caspian and the mounting evidence against him.

"Big Bib?" I asked, knowing he'd be able to tell me. Big Bib never forgot a face.

"Beard, overalls, really plays the part of mechanic." Caspian observed but did not realize Big Bib was not an actor playing a part. He reached down into his pocket and took out his phone.

He hit the screen like a text had come in.

"I've got to go. It seems like your sheriff is also very interested in what I was doing the night Leandar died. I will leave."

Despite his attempts to explain away my questions, I couldn't shake the feeling that something was off. I knew I needed to dig deeper, gather more information, and uncover the truth about what had happened to Leandar.

The future of Honey Springs and the safety of its residents were at stake, and I was determined to get to the bottom of it, no matter the cost.

CHAPTER SIXTEEN

As Patrick and I returned home to our cozy cabin, the sky was awash with the soft hues of dusk. We entered the living room and settled down on the couch, the warm glow of the fireplace casting flickering shadows on the walls.

Sassy and Pepper wagged their tails and jumped around us, excited to see us home after our tense meeting with Caspian at Aunt Maxi's old house.

"All right, you two," I said with a chuckle. "Let's get you outside for a potty break."

Patrick held the door and ushered Sassy and Pepper out into the front yard, where they immediately began sniffing around and exploring.

We stood there for a moment, watching them play and enjoying the fresh air as the sun dipped lower in the sky, casting a warm golden glow over everything.

When the dogs were content, we called them back inside, and I headed into the kitchen to prepare some snacks for us to enjoy. I rummaged through the cabinets, gathering an assortment of crackers, cheese, and sliced meats to create a small charcuterie board.

As I arranged the snacks on a wooden platter, Patrick grabbed a bottle of wine from the rack and began to uncork it.

"Here, let me help you with that," I said, taking the corkscrew from him and expertly freeing the cork from the bottle.

He grinned at me, his eyes twinkling with amusement. "You've always been the wine expert in this relationship."

"And coffee expert." I smiled and gave him a quick kiss.

With the bottle uncorked, Patrick fetched two wineglasses from the cupboard while I finished arranging the snacks. We carried our impromptu feast into the living room, setting everything down on the coffee table before settling onto the couch.

Patrick's expression was a mix of concern and frustration as he turned to face me. "Roxy, I can't believe you confronted Caspian like that. What if he really had killed Leandar? You could've put yourself in serious danger."

I sighed, feeling both guilty and defensive. "I know, Patrick, but I couldn't just sit there and not ask the questions that needed to be asked. We needed to know the truth about Caspian's involvement."

His eyes softened, but the worry remained. "I understand that, Roxy, but I can't stand the thought of anything happening to you. I love you so much, and the idea of losing you... It's unbearable."

I felt tears prick at the corners of my eyes as I reached out to take his hand. "I love you, too, Patrick, more than anything. I promise I'll be more careful in the future."

He pulled me into a tight embrace, burying his face in my hair. "I just want to keep you safe, Roxy. You mean the world to me."

As we held each other, Pepper jumped up onto the couch and snuggled between us, wagging his tail and seeking our attention. We laughed through our tears, the tension between us dissipating as we focused on the love and happiness we shared.

Patrick gently tilted my chin up, his eyes locked onto mine. "I'll always be here for you, Roxy, no matter what."

I smiled, my heart swelling with love for this wonderful man who had been my rock through thick and thin. "And I'll always be here for you, Patrick."

As our lips met in a tender, passionate kiss, the sun dipped below the horizon outside our cabin window. Our love shone brightly in the midst of uncertainty and fear, a beacon of hope and strength to guide us through whatever challenges the future held.

As Patrick and I sat on the couch, entwined in each other's arms and surrounded by the love of our little family, we began to discuss our shared love for Honey Springs.

"You know, Patrick," I said, my voice soft with affection, "I can't imagine a better place to call home than Honey Springs. There's just something so special about this small town in addition to me meeting you here."

He nodded, his eyes taking on a distant, dreamy quality. "I couldn't agree more, Roxy. The sense of community, the natural beauty, the charm of our little shops and cafés... It's all so incredible. Even growing up here, I never had the urge to move away."

"I just hope that the development of the country club won't change Honey Springs too much," I mused, my brow furrowing with concern. "I mean, it's bound to bring more tourism and employment opportunities, which is great, but I don't want our town to lose its soul in the process."

Patrick hugged me tighter, his warmth reassuring. "I know what you mean, Roxy. But we'll do everything we can to preserve the essence of Honey Springs. We'll work with the community and make sure that any development is done with sensitivity and respect for our town's history and traditions."

I smiled at his optimism and determination. "That's one of the many things I love about you, Patrick. Your commitment to our town and its people is so inspiring."

He brushed a strand of hair from my face, his eyes filled with love. "And I love your passion for justice and your dedication to protecting the people of Honey Springs. Together, we'll make sure that our town remains the beautiful, welcoming place we know and love."

Patrick's phone rang.

It was Franny, Patrick's secretary.

"Wonder what she wants so late." He had a funny look but accepted the call. "Hey, Franny. I've got you on speakerphone with Roxy here. Is everything okay?"

"Okay? It's more than okay!" she screamed. "Patrick! Roxy! I'm so sorry to bother you after hours, but I just couldn't wait to tell you the news!" she gushed.

"What's going on, Franny?" Patrick asked, his curiosity piqued.

"We got it! We got the bid for the new country club! Cane Construction is going to build it!" she exclaimed, barely able to contain her excitement.

Patrick's eyes widened, and he exchanged a thrilled glance with me. "That's incredible news, Franny! Thank you so much for letting us know."

"Yeah, Franny, this is fantastic!" I chimed in, my heart swelling with pride for Patrick and his team. I had no idea he'd even put in for the bid. "We really appreciate you calling to tell us."

Franny's voice softened, but the excitement was still palpable. "I just couldn't wait until tomorrow. This is such a huge deal for Cane Construction, and I wanted you two to know as soon as possible. Congratulations!"

"Thank you, Franny. We'll celebrate this accomplishment at the office tomorrow," Patrick promised.

After saying our goodbyes and ending the call, Patrick and I looked at each other, still processing the incredible news.

"Can you believe it, Roxy?" Patrick asked, his voice filled with wonder. "Our company is going to build the new country club. This is going to be huge for us!"

I reached over and squeezed his hand, my eyes shining with pride. "I knew you could do it, Patrick. This is going to be amazing for Cane Construction and for Honey Springs."

We clinked our wineglasses together, toasting our success and the bright future that lay ahead for our town and our business. With love, determination, and a shared vision, we knew that we could help shape Honey Springs into a thriving, vibrant community that would continue to grow and prosper.

But in the back of my head—and it stayed there though I would further investigate later—was it me, or was it just coincidence that we'd just met with Caspian, sold Aunt Maxi's old house to him, and confronted him about his possible involvement about Leandar's death, and *then* Cane Construction got the bid at this hour?

It would go right along with the information I'd found on the internet about Blackwood Associates's shady deals.

CHAPTER SEVENTEEN

I stood behind the counter at the Bean Hive, the early morning sun streaming through the windows and casting a warm golden glow over the lake outside.

The aroma of freshly brewed coffee filled the air, its comforting scent promising a perfect start to the day.

Danielle was coming in this morning to pick up Jessie before we opened. She'd made it official that she was going to adopt the cute pup and take him home to live with her.

It was funny how friendships formed. Though she didn't live in Honey Springs, we'd been able to form a bond between us in the most unexpected of circumstances. It was a friendship I was sure was going to last.

I had already gotten the adoption papers ready, so when she came in they were ready for her to sign. Jessie knew something was up. He was prancing around all by himself, not following Pepper like he'd done since Louise had dropped him off. It was a sign he was ready to be the dog of his own domain.

"It looks like we are all out of leads." I sat little Jessie's bag of toys and the packet Louise Carlton had left for him when she dropped him off to be the featured animal from the Pet Palace.

"I can say my time here in Honey Springs has definitely been one to remember." Danielle looked a whole lot better than the last time I'd talked with her. "Now that the new development doesn't require me to do any more environmental testing for Blackwood Associates, I think I'm going to find a different job."

"Oh yeah?" I had a pit in my stomach from signing the papers for Aunt Maxi's house over to Caspian Blackwood for the new country-club development.

It was good. I had to remember that it was best for Honey Springs. There was more lakefront property and beach than any old development. It was the development that would help spur more tourists to visit here, and it was going to be a great way to show off our gorgeous little part of Kentucky.

"What do you have in mind?" I asked her and tucked the official adoption papers under my arm as I got us two cups of freshly brewed hot coffee.

"I'm not sure. Where I live, we have the ocean, mountains, and forest, so I'm sure I can find something there," she said. "You should come visit. I think you'd like it."

"Where do you live?" I asked.

"It's a small town out west called Holiday Junction." She picked Jessie up and nuzzled him. "He is going to love all the walks. We even have a dog that's the mayor. Mayor Paisley."

"A dog?" I snorted.

"Yes, but I'm thinking Jessie might give her a run for her money next election." She winked. "Where do I sign?"

She put Jessie down so she could sign the papers to make it official.

As Danielle signed the adoption papers, Jessie wagged his tail excitedly, his little body practically quivering with joy.

Pepper was going to miss having Jessie around as a playmate at the Bean Hive, but seeing the love and happiness on Danielle's face made it all worthwhile.

"Roxy, I just wanted to thank you," Danielle began, her eyes filling with gratitude. "Not only for being my lawyer when Spencer thought I killed Leandar, but also for your friendship. You stood by me when so many others turned their backs."

I smiled warmly, my heart swelling with pride and affection. "That's what friends do, Danielle. I'm just glad we were able to prove your innocence."

As we shared a quiet, heartfelt moment, a sudden blur of movement outside the window caught our attention. A man sprinted past on the boardwalk, his pace steady and determined. Danielle watched him go, a thoughtful expression on her face.

"You know," she said, her gaze following the runner, "that guy runs by here every day. He even stopped to chat with me once. He mentioned something about the land development Leandar was involved in and how it had ruined his family."

"Oh really?" I got up and tried to look out the window, but the runner was gone. "Where did you run into him?"

"The little antique store down the boardwalk. He was bringing the owners some of his family's bone china. The owners were so excited about it." She had to be talking about Caldwell Featherstone.

"Did he tell you why he thought Leandar had ruined their family?" I asked.

"He wasn't talking to me. He was telling the owners how they still had to sell the china in order to get hay for their livestock or something like that. I overheard them." She looked around and said, "You know, the china he brought in would go great with your décor."

"Yes, it would." I kept to myself how I had planned on buying that china at the estate auction that never was, but I couldn't keep to myself who he was. "I bet it was Caldwell Featherstone."

"Any relation to Raffery Featherstone? One of the golf course investors?" she asked and took the last sip of coffee.

"His son." I tried to recall the conversation I'd had with him on the boat that night, but the sun was up, and the first customer was at the door, waiting for me to unlock it.

It was Bunny's day off, so it was just me in the Bean Hive this morning, which meant any notion I had to go question Caldwell about what he'd said in passing to the Teagardens was going to have to wait until the afternoon staff came.

Even when Danielle and Jessie left, she didn't take with her the thoughts I'd gotten when she ID'd the runner.

What if Raffery Featherstone really did kill Leandar? He had a very shoddy alibi with the jug fishing.

The more the morning dragged on, I started to recall some of the conversation about how Caldwell knew the time because he was playing video games online with buddies. Not realizing it, he really did put his father at the scene of the crime.

A shiver ran down my spine, realization dawning on me. Could Caldwell be the real killer?

I might have just stumbled upon the key to solving Leandar's murder.

There was only one way to find out which Featherstone had killed Leandar, and that was going right back to the Featherstone farm and doing a little more snooping around, this time without Spencer.

CHAPTER EIGHTEEN

Before I went, I decided to take all the knowledge I was armed with about Caldwell's little visit to Wild and Whimsy, thanks to what Danielle had told me. I decided to stop by the antique shop to talk to Beverly Teagarden myself to see what she had to say about the conversation.

The one sure way to get Beverly to open up was to make and take her one of her favorite breads that just so happened to be in season: honeysuckle-infused bread. We in Kentucky called it Appalachia summer bread.

I'd already made the honeysuckle syrup when the honeysuckle trees had bloomed in early spring. It was a tedious job to pick all the flowering buds and boil them down to the syrup, but it was one of those things I did on Sundays when I took advantage of the coffee shop being closed during the winter and early spring months.

Since it was the lull time between the lunch rush and the afternoon customers, I was able to prop the swinging door between the coffee shop and the kitchen open. I couldn't risk the health department coming in and shutting me down, so I had to work fast.

I grabbed all the dry ingredients off the shelf and put them on the kitchen workstation before I went to the refrigerator for the wet ingredients.

Since the bread was a staple in my life growing up due to the fact that we had so many honeysuckle trees, I was really good at eyeballing the ingredients instead of going straight from the recipe.

With my oven set on preheat, I retrieved the stand mixer from one of the shelves underneath the workstation and started to add the flour, baking soda, oils, salt, buttermilk, lemon zest, eggs, and the final touch —the homemade honeysuckle syrup.

With everything all married together, I put the mixture in a few glass bread-baking dishes and placed it in the oven.

It didn't take long before the sweet aroma of the baking bread, infused with the delicate sweetness of honeysuckle, brought back memories of countless summers spent in Honey Springs, surrounded by the gentle fragrance of blossoming flowers.

It was Aunt Maxi's recipe that was baked into my head and beloved by all.

The tantalizing smell of the bread mingled with the rich, earthy aroma of freshly ground coffee beans, creating an irresistible blend of scents that permeated every corner of the cozy kitchen. The familiar smell of butter and sugar caramelizing in the oven filled the air as the bread baked to golden perfection.

As I inhaled the delightful medley of scents, I felt a wave of contentment wash over me.

The kitchen was my sanctuary, a place where I could lose myself in the simple pleasure of creating delicious treats for others to enjoy and forget about why I was making the bread in the first place.

Still, Leandar's murder wasn't too far buried in the back of my head.

While the loaves of bread baked, I made sure everything inside the coffee shop was stocked so the Riddle twins didn't have to worry about anything. I'd even had time to get the morning industrial coffeepots ready, which was now on the afternoon employees' list of things to do.

It wasn't too long after the timers for the oven went off that the twins got there for their afternoon shift, allowing me to leave a little earlier than normal.

"Afternoon!" Beverly greeted me as soon as the bell over the door chimed and she recognized it was me. "You better not walk any further unless you've got something in your hands."

I lifted up the bag with the Appalachian honeysuckle bread in it.

"Do you think I'd do that to you? Especially if I've got a loaf of Appalachian honeysuckle bread you love in here?" I wagged the bag as I walked through the store to the check-out counter where Beverly was using the handheld pricing machine to stick the price on some of the new antiques they'd gotten.

I set the bag on the counter.

"How are Savannah and Melanie?" I asked and looked around the shop to see if they were there. "I do have a couple extra mini-loaves in there for them." I winked when I saw they weren't around.

"Do we have to tell them?" she joked. "And Dan is outside working on the awning, so when you leave, don't tell him about these either."

Beverly had already taken one out and bit into it, humming happily with each chew.

"I didn't see him when I came in." I would've noticed since I'd walked right under the awning where the sign that read Wild and Whimsy dangled down.

"There's a few rusty bolts where he had to screw the awning on the tin roof," she muttered under another bite. "He probably had to run to the hardware store."

"Ah." I nodded.

"So." Beverly gave me the side eye. "What are you doing here this time of the day? And with my favorite seasonal bread?"

"You know me all too well." There was no pulling the wool over her eyes. "Two things. How much for the Featherstones' bone china?"

Beverly laughed.

"And can you tell me about the conversation you had with Caldwell Featherstone when he dropped off the china?"

Now, that threw her for a loop.

"Why? Is Caldwell in trouble?" she asked.

"No." I shook my head. "I'm doing a little double-dipping with Spencer by keeping my ear to the ground if I hear any information and also representing Danielle Quillen, the environmentalist in town, as a suspect in Leandar's murder. And she happened to mention how she overheard Caldwell in here talking about his family."

"You know kids." Beverly pooh-poohed the conversation. It was her way of not getting involved or gossiping. "Caldwell was talking to me and the girls. They are the same age and went to high school together."

"I know. He said he remembered me from teaching their home economics class that time." I laughed.

"Anyways, I'd asked him about how his parents were doing with selling, and that's when he said they'd decided not to sell because Leandar's little scheme messed them up." She used the word "scheme," which was very interesting.

"Scheme?" I asked to make sure.

"You know kids. I'm sure he'd heard it from Raffery and was just repeating. But when I asked about why he was bringing the china in, he said his mom told him they needed the money because they'd not gotten enough hay or feed for the horses since they thought the new owners would take over." She tsked and frowned.

"Were they having financial problems?" I asked.

"One of my girls said she'd heard they had a hard time paying the mortgage, so when Blackwood Associates was looking for investors, Caldwell told her how Raffery had jumped on it. Not only would selling the farm give them enough to invest, but also the cost of a small townhome at the country club would be paid off, as well as a lifetime membership to the country club." Beverly didn't know it, but what she just told me gave me plenty of motives and reasons for Raffery to have killed Leandar out of anger.

"That's too bad." I shook my head, keeping my thoughts to myself. "How about the price of that china?"

Beverly never gave me the price. She said she'd let me know, and I'd have first option to buy, which I fully intended to do.

There was one more person I needed to visit before I went home for the night.

Raffery Featherstone.

As I drove along the old, winding roads in the late afternoon, I couldn't help but marvel at the beauty of the Kentucky countryside. The Hill Dairy Farm, with its gently rolling hills and lush pastures, was a testament to the bluegrass region's rich agricultural heritage. The sun cast a warm golden light on the fields, making the vibrant green grass appear to glow with life.

Eventually, I arrived at the Featherstone farm, an impressive estate known for its prized racehorses. The sprawling property was undoubtedly worth a fortune, but I knew that maintaining such a place came with considerable costs. When the development deal fell through, the Featherstones found themselves in dire financial straits—at least, that's the conclusion I came to after visiting with Beverly Teagarden.

She'd confided in me that the Featherstones were struggling with mortgage payments, which was why they were hosting an estate sale. The sale of their belongings would allow them to purchase a nice condo within the country club, offering them a more manageable lifestyle.

I was there to talk to Raffery Featherstone about his potential involvement in Leandar's murder. His late-night jug fishing put him at the scene, but with the discovery of a second murder location, I needed to find out where Raffery had been right after the emergency meeting where the development was voted down. Had he killed Leandar in a fit of rage?

When I arrived at their home, Caldwell, Raffery's son, let me in.

"They aren't here. I think they went to the bank to meet with that developer." Caldwell stood inside the entry.

In the background, I could hear the sound of muffled voices. Was Raffery there and Caldwell covering for his father?

After all, Caldwell was the gamer.

"Do you know how long they will be?" I asked and moved past him to look into the other room where the noise was coming from.

"No," Caldwell said. "I'll go grab a piece of paper from Dad's office, and you can write a note. If you don't, I might forget you stopped by."

Caldwell left the room. I heard someone over the earphones attached to the gaming console, yelling for Raffery to play.

Picking up the earphones, I listened for a moment.

"Raffery, man, come on. You're going to get us killed," one of the other players said, confirming they thought it was Raffery playing, not Caldwell. This revelation didn't make sense to me at first, but the pieces began to fall into place as I continued to survey the room.

I had been transported back to the dinner cruise when Caldwell had told me how he was playing video games in the middle of the night and early morning when Leandar was murdered and his dad had come in from jug fishing.

Was it the other way around?

The other gamers continued to yell for Raffery to move in what appeared to be a game where they all played together in order to advance. I picked up the remote.

My eyes fell on a small amount of what looked like a smear of blood on the corner of the remote control where the fatty part of the thumb would lay.

I scanned the room and noticed a baseball bat in the corner.

It suddenly became clear to me that Caldwell was the one who had hit Leandar on the head right here in this home.

It was possible that he'd taken Leandar to the beach to be found. It was Danielle who had ID'd Caldwell earlier when he was jogging past the Bean Hive.

He'd called the sheriff, pretending to have stumbled upon the body while out running.

As the chilling truth dawned on me, I realized I needed to confront Caldwell and uncover the full extent of his involvement in Leandar's murder. I couldn't let an innocent man take the blame for a crime he didn't commit, and I was determined to see justice served.

I took a deep breath as I approached Caldwell, my heart pounding with a mixture of anxiety and determination. It was time to confront him about Leandar's murder, and I had to know the truth.

"Caldwell," I began, my voice steady despite the storm of emotions swirling within me, "I need to talk to you about what happened the night Leandar died."

He tensed, his eyes widening in surprise and fear. It was clear that he hadn't expected me to discover his secret.

"I know you were the one who killed him, Caldwell," I continued, watching as his face turned pale. "But I also know that you didn't mean to do it. I believe you thought he was an intruder."

Caldwell stared at me, his eyes filled with a mixture of relief and desperation. "Roxy, I swear, I didn't mean to kill anyone. I was just playing my video game, and when I saw his reflection on the TV screen, I panicked. I thought someone had broken into our home, and I was just trying to protect myself and our house."

His voice trembled, and I could see the weight of his guilt and fear pressing down upon him. "I didn't know it was Leandar until it was too late," he added, his eyes brimming with tears. "I didn't know what to do, so I took his body to the lake, hoping it would buy me some time to figure things out."

As I listened to his confession, I felt a swell of sympathy for Caldwell. He had made a tragic mistake, driven by fear and a desire to protect his home and family. It was clear that he was haunted by his actions, and the burden of his secret had become almost too much to bear.

"Caldwell," I said gently, "you need to come forward and tell the truth. It's the only way to start making things right. I know you didn't mean for any of this to happen, but it's important to take responsibility for your actions."

He nodded slowly, tears streaming down his face as he finally surrendered to the weight of his guilt. "You're right, Roxy," he whispered. "I'll tell the truth. I just hope everyone can understand that I never meant for any of this to happen."

As I stood by his side, ready to support him as he faced the consequences of his actions, I knew that the road ahead would be difficult for both Caldwell and the entire community of Honey Springs. But I also believed that through honesty, understanding, and compassion, we would find a way to heal and move forward together.

But I knew we had to call Sheriff Spencer Shephard.

I took out my cell phone, dialed Sheriff Spencer's number, and waited for him to pick up. "Sheriff, it's Roxy. I'm here with Caldwell, and he has something important to tell you."

I handed the phone to Caldwell, whose hands were trembling as he took it from me. He hesitated for a moment, taking a deep breath before speaking. "Sheriff Spencer, it's Caldwell Featherstone. I... I need to confess something."

There was a pause as he listened to the sheriff's response, his eyes flicking to me for reassurance. I gave him an encouraging nod, urging him to continue.

"I was the one who killed Leandar," he admitted, his voice cracking. "But it was an accident. I thought he was an intruder when I saw his reflection on the TV screen. I panicked and hit him with a bat. I never meant for any of this to happen."

Silence filled the room as Caldwell listened to Sheriff Spencer's response. It was clear that the sheriff was taken aback by the confession, but his voice remained calm and professional as he instructed Caldwell on the next steps.

After a few more minutes of conversation, Caldwell hung up the phone and handed it back to me, his face etched with a mixture of relief and anxiety. "He said I should come down to the sheriff's department right away to make an official statement."

He paused for a moment, his eyes pleading. "Roxy, would you come with me? I don't think I can face this alone."

"Of course, Caldwell," I replied, placing a comforting hand on his shoulder. "I'll be there with you every step of the way."

We left the Featherstone home and headed toward the sheriff's department. But as we walked side by side, I was reminded of the power of truth, compassion, and support to help guide us through even the darkest of times.

As Caldwell and I entered the sheriff's department, Sheriff Spencer and Caldwell's parents were waiting for us. Spencer must've called them to let them know what Caldwell had confessed to.

Spencer's expression was a mix of sympathy and professionalism. He gestured for us to sit down in a couple of chairs across from his desk, and we obliged.

"Thank you for coming in, Caldwell," he began, his voice firm but gentle. "It takes a lot of courage to face the consequences of your actions, especially when they've had such tragic results."

Caldwell swallowed hard, nodding in acknowledgment. "I know I can't undo what's happened, but I want to do whatever I can to make things right."

Spencer nodded, his eyes meeting Caldwell's. "First, we'll need to take a formal statement from you. I'll ask you to recount the events leading up to and following Leandar's death, and we'll have a deputy transcribe your words. This statement will become part of the official record."

Caldwell nodded, his hands fidgeting nervously in his lap. "Okay, I understand."

"Once we have your statement," Spencer continued, "we'll need to investigate further. This includes gathering any additional evidence, speaking with witnesses, and corroborating your version of events. We'll also need to consult with the district attorney to determine the appropriate charges."

Caldwell's eyes widened with fear, but he didn't protest. "I'll cooperate fully with the investigation," he promised.

Spencer softened his expression slightly. "I appreciate that, Caldwell. And remember, you have the right to legal counsel throughout this process. I recommend you get in touch with a lawyer as soon as possible to ensure your rights are protected."

Caldwell looked at me, his eyes pleading. "Roxy, would you consider representing me?"

I hesitated for a moment, weighing the gravity of the situation. Then, I nodded. "I'll do my best to help you through this, Caldwell."

With my support, and the guidance of Spencer, we began the difficult process of addressing the consequences of Caldwell's actions. Although the road ahead was uncertain, we were committed to seeking justice and healing for all those affected by this tragic event.

CHAPTER NINETEEN

The next day was difficult for Honey Springs.

One of our own was dead. Though Leandar Taylor was shifty at times, he was still ours. And one of our own was his killer.

I recalled standing in the Featherstones' living room the day before and talking with Caldwell after he'd been given the appropriate charges, the shocking truth about Leandar's murder finally becoming clear.

Caldwell had come home from college early, unaware of the events that had transpired during the emergency meeting. He had been at home, immersed in a video game with his headset on, completely oblivious to the world outside.

Leandar, having not yet received Raffery Featherstone's emails and voicemails about removing the farm from the market and canceling the estate sale, had used his key as the Realtor to enter the house and check if it was ready for the upcoming event.

When no one answered his knock on the door, he went inside, unknowingly setting off a tragic chain of events. Raffery and his wife hadn't gone straight home after the meeting, so they had no idea this had taken place. When they did get home, Raffery did go jug fishing, just like Caldwell had told me.

Caldwell, startled by the unexpected intruder, caught a glimpse of Leandar's reflection on the television screen. In a moment of panic, he dropped the game remote, grabbed a nearby bat, and swung it with all his might, striking Leandar in the head and killing him instantly.

Overwhelmed by fear, Caldwell hastily transported Leandar's body to the lake, where he later called the sheriff, pretending to have stumbled upon the body during a nighttime run. When he returned home, his parents were there, but they had no idea what had transpired. Caldwell had carefully concealed any signs of the incident, replacing the bat and resuming his video game as if nothing had happened.

But he hadn't noticed the small amount of blood that had transferred from his hands to the remote, a crucial piece of evidence that I had spotted when I came to confront Raffery about the murder. It was that seemingly insignificant detail that had allowed me to put the pieces together and uncover the truth about Caldwell's involvement in Leandar's tragic death.

As I stood behind the counter of the Bean Hive, reflecting on the devastating series of events and the lives that had been forever changed, I felt a mixture of relief and sorrow.

We had finally solved Leandar's murder, but at what cost?

The weight of the truth weighed heavily on my heart, a stark reminder that life could be irrevocably altered in the blink of an eye and that sometimes the most heartbreaking truths lay hidden beneath the surface.

I took solace in knowing the Bean Hive was more than just a place for people to enjoy coffee and delicious treats; it was a haven where people could come together, share their thoughts and emotions, and find support in one another. It was a testament to the resilience and strength of the Honey Springs community that, even in the face of tragedy, they were able to rally together and find solace in each other's company.

As I continued to serve my customers and listen to their stories, I was reminded of the importance of human connection, especially during trying times. People from all walks of life found their way to the

Bean Hive, united by their shared experiences, grief, and hope for healing.

In the weeks that followed, the Bean Hive became a beacon of light for the people of Honey Springs. The laughter, tears, and heartfelt conversations shared within its walls spoke to the power of community and the unbreakable bonds that held us together.

Through it all, I found my own sense of purpose and fulfillment in providing a space where people could find comfort and healing. The Bean Hive had become more than just a coffee shop; it was a symbol of the enduring spirit of Honey Springs, a place where people could come together and face even the darkest of times with hope, love, and unity.

As I glanced around the coffee shop, my eyes fell upon Aunt Maxi, Patrick, my mama, and Bunny, all engrossed in a lively conversation about the new development of the country club. Their excitement was palpable, and it was clear that they believed the project would bring about positive change and prosperity for Honey Springs.

Not only had they posted the building plans for the development in the courthouse for everyone to see, but also they'd decided on keeping Aunt Maxi's house for the main building of the country club where events could be hosted.

After all, it had the most beautiful view of the lake and was a grand place to have an event.

However, as I observed their animated discussion, I couldn't help but feel a twinge of uncertainty.

The country club would no doubt boost tourism and create job opportunities, but at what cost? How much would Honey Springs change in the process? Would the tight-knit community I had come to love and cherish still retain its charm and warmth, or would it be transformed beyond recognition?

As I pondered these thoughts, I realized that change was inevitable and that progress often came with its own set of challenges. Yet it was in the face of change that the people of Honey Springs had always displayed their resilience, adapting and coming together to ensure the well-being of their community.

With the Bean Hive as a cornerstone of the community, I resolved to do my part in keeping the essence of Honey Springs alive and thriving, even as the town embarked on a new chapter of growth and development.

I stood behind the counter, using a wet towel to clean and dry my new Featherstone bone china. Beverly Teagarden had sold it to me for the price she could've gotten if she'd sold it in the store.

I couldn't help but think about the one thing I knew for sure.

The Bean Hive was more than just a coffee shop; it was a place where people could gather, connect, and find comfort in the simple pleasures of life, like the aroma of fresh honeysuckle bread wafting through the air.

And no development would change that.

THE END

If you enjoyed reading this book as much as I enjoyed writing it then be sure to return to the Amazon page and leave a review.

Go to Tonyakappes.com for a full reading order of my novels and while there join my newsletter. You can also find links to Facebook, Instagram and Goodreads.

Macchiato Murder, book 13 in Killer Coffee Cozy Mystery is now available on Amazon. You don't want to miss this Halloween edition to the series that'll keep you guessing until the end. Keep reading for a sneak peek!

Chapter One of Book Thirteen
Macchiato Murder

The spirit of Halloween wafted through the coffee shop, filling hearts with excitement. Neewollah Festival, our town's annual, beloved celebration of all things autumn, was in full swing.

As the morning sun bathed the boardwalk in a gentle glow, I soaked in the magic of the season seeping through the café walls. The cozy atmosphere spilled out with the laughter of friends who were walking in the door of the Bean Hive Coffee Shop.

"Good morning." I greeted them as I did every single customer who walked through my coffee-shop door. "Y'all enjoying the festival activities so far?" I asked and ushered them to a table near the front of the coffee shop so they could enjoy their morning coffee with the amazing views of Lake Honey Springs and the fall colors that had painted the trees wrapping around the lake.

"Of course, they are going to the festival." Eleanor Blackthorn sidled up behind me. She reached around me and put a flyer on the table. "And I sure hope you come to Hollow Manor."

Eleanor, our spirited historian, had her sights set on breathing new life into the old farm mansion on the outskirts of town. She had a knack for exaggeration, often spinning tales of mythical creatures and haunted happenings. The running joke was how you had to take whatever Eleanor said and cut it in half to get to the truth.

And after she'd inherited the old mansion and told everyone in town how she was going to get it in the historic registry, everyone, including me, had our doubts.

We were all surprised when she did put together a plan and worked over the last few months with Babette Cliff, an event planner who owned All About the Detail.

"We have something for everyone." Eleanor had a flair for being over the top. Even more than my aunt Maxine Bloom.

And that was saying something.

Eleanor had a wild mane of silver-streaked hair that seemed to have a life of its own. She truly embodied the word "eccentric." Her wardrobe was an explosion of colors, patterns, and textures, with flowing skirts, mismatched socks, and an array of whimsical accessories. Each piece she wore told a story, reflecting her free-spirited nature and love for all things unique.

No wonder she and Aunt Maxi had been lifelong friends. When I was a child and visited Aunt Maxi every summer, one of my favorite activities was going to visit Eleanor with Aunt Maxi. I would sit and listen to her tell big tales about the town's history and folklore. However, she often added her own imaginative twists to the tales, weaving elaborate stories of mythical creatures and supernatural happenings. At least, that's what Aunt Maxi would tell me when we'd get back in the car and I'd be daydreaming of all the stories Eleanor had told me.

"You have to get there early today and pick a pumpkin from the Pumpkin Patch." She pointed to the flyer that listed all the activities for Hollow Mansion. "There's a carving station that's open until five p.m., then you can take your pumpkin over to the judging tables. The winner will be announced at nine p.m. after the big magic show."

"Thank you," I interrupted Eleanor politely. "Let me get them caffeinated so they can participate today."

It was my way of not disrespecting Eleanor as one of my elders but still making sure my customers were taken care of.

"What can I get you started off with?" I asked and didn't bother writing down what the four of them had ordered, mentally repeating their order in my head as they gave it to me. "While I get your orders made, you're more than welcome to check out the menu."

I pointed out the four large chalkboards that hung down from the ceiling over the L-shaped glass countertop.

The first chalkboard menu hung over the pie counter and listed the pies and cookies with their prices. The second menu hung over the tortes and quiches. The third menu before the L-shaped counter curved listed the breakfast casseroles and drinks. Over top the other counter, the chalkboard listed lunch options, including soups, and catering information.

"We have a variety of homemade pastries today, and you can read those over the first chalkboard. As you can see, they are all holiday themed for the festival," I told them and smiled as I pointed out the tasty treats. "You check out the list, and I'll be right back."

Wicked Witch Cupcakes were very rich chocolate cupcakes topped with vibrant green buttercream frosting and a candy witch hat garnish that one of the twins, Shelley and Shanda Riddle, had thought up when we were brainstorming about what we could offer to go with the coffee. They were amazing young women who worked at the Bean Hive after school, on weekends, and on holidays.

Spooky Spiderweb Donuts were fluffy donuts drizzled with a delicate white glaze in a spiderweb pattern, adorned with a chocolate spider that was so darling.

Pumpkin Patch Pies were mini hand pies with a buttery crust and a hint of pumpkin spice, sprinkled with cinnamon and nutmeg, and shaped like tiny pumpkins.

Haunted House Brownies were truly decadent chocolate brownies topped with black icing to resemble a spooky haunted house, complete with ghostly marshmallow shapes.

Shanda's favorite was the Monster Mash Cookie that she'd come up with. It was a colorful sugar cookie decorated with edible monster faces, featuring googly eyes and mismatched icing. Out of the two, she was the more creative when it came to decorating.

Then, for our more traditional customers, we offered what we were calling the Graveyard Cheesecake Bars, a creamy cheesecake bar on a crumbly chocolate cookie crust, topped with cookie tombstones and gummy worms.

Then I turned our usual macarons into Candy Corn Macarons, delicate, almond-flavored, and filled with a sweet, candy corn-flavored buttercream, capturing the iconic Halloween candy's colors.

Of course, Bunny had to put her two cents in because she loved my homemade cinnamon rolls. They were easy enough to make into

Vampire Bites, where I drizzled a little bloodred glaze on top for a delightfully spooky twist.

I kept the scones the same because they were already perfection, if I had to say so myself. We just changed the name to Witch's Brew Scones and then paired them with our Witch's Brew Coffee blend.

We had something for everyone, and coming up with all of it made this year's festival even more fun.

As I left the table with their coffee order in my mind, Eleanor continued right where she left off.

"The last time the Hollow Mansion was open was over fifty years ago when the then-owners had a Halloween party with a magician. Only the curse of Hollow Mansion killed the magician, and it's been haunted since." I heard her and looked over my shoulder to see the reaction of the customers.

Eleanor's eyes, bright and sparkling with curiosity, held a hint of mischief and a touch of mystery as she continued to tell them about the old wives' tale that'd never been proven.

Her hands twisted in the air, and her eyes seemed to dance with an inner light, making me think she really did believe the old run-down mansion was haunted.

Her voice, as she spun her tales and shared her ambitious plans, was filled with enthusiasm and an infectious energy that had drawn the customers in.

"She's bad for business," Bunny scoffed when I walked behind the glass counter, where she was boxing up a few of the Spooky Spiderweb Donuts. "She sounds crazy." Bunny's brows knotted. Her gray hair, parted to the side and cut at chin length, framed her worried face.

"She's harmless," I said to keep the peace. "Look at them." I tossed a chin toward the group as I started to make the murdery macchiato concoction, which was literally the basic macchiato with a festive name change for the holiday. "They are enthralled by her story."

"They are enthralled by her crazy." Bunny lifted her crooked pointer finger up to her ear and started to gesture the crazy sign, making me laugh. "It's your coffee shop. I'm just here to help out."

Bunny Bowowski had been what she called "helping out" since the first week I'd opened the Bean Hive. She and her best friend, Mae Belle Donovan, were my first ever customers that'd made it a morning ritual to hold their gossip session in one of the few café tables that dotted the inside of the cozy shop.

Many times I'd sit at one of the two long window tables with stools butted up to them on each side of the front door while they sipped and gossiped, just waiting for more customers to come in.

It was a time during the revitalization of the boardwalk and Honey Springs itself where the Southern Woman's Club, along with the town council, had spent a lot of time and effort to grow the economy by putting money into tourism.

Luckily, Aunt Maxi owned the building, and the recent tenants had a restaurant that'd folded, making it easy for something like the coffee shop to move right on in.

I'd found myself at that same time building my new life as a recent divorcee, where I'd fled life as a lawyer to find comfort in the one place that had embraced me like a warm, fuzzy blanket.

Aunt Maxi's and this little lake town.

Though I wasn't from Honey Springs or technically grew up there, every summer as soon as my dad's car would cross the county line, I felt like I was coming home. I was a kid, but I knew my feelings. Every year when summer was over, it felt like a part of my soul had been ripped out of my body.

So naturally, when my soul needed healing for me to live again, I found myself in Honey Springs, opening up a coffee shop and reconnecting with the then-teenage boy I'd fallen in love with during the long, summer lake nights.

Patrick Cane.

"See? Look at her." Bunny smacked the back of her hand on my arm, flinging the crooked finger back to Eleanor, who had found another group coming in the door to hand her flyer to. "Crazy with a capital C. Did you hear me?"

"Yes. I heard you. But I was thinking back to when I was a kid, and I could sit and listen to Eleanor for hours." I shrugged off Bunny's concern. She made quite obvious by her *harrumph* that she didn't like my response.

"Like I said, I'm only here to help you out," she said again and handed me a small serving tray for the drinks.

"Then you don't want this?" I turned and plucked an envelope with her paycheck in it from the stack next to the register.

"I didn't say that, now." Bunny snapped it out of my hand, folded it, and put it in the apron she'd tied around the waist of her housecoat, her usual dress attire even though we had uniform shirts with the Bean Hive's logo on them.

With the drinks on the tray, I headed back to the customers where they'd decided to enjoy their coffee without anything to eat.

As I made my way around the bustling café, I engaged in lively conversations with our other patrons, eager to ensure their every need was met.

"Is there anything else I can get for you?" I asked, my voice filled with genuine warmth and hospitality. The laughter and animated chatter echoed against the walls as friends gathered to savor moments of connection in the midst of their busy lives.

I picked up some paper wrappers and empty cups along the way, tossing what I could in the trash and the recycle bins as I made my way over to the fireplace.

"You just tell him to move if he's bothering you." I pointed to Pepper, my furry schnauzer companion, who thought of the coffee shop as his second home.

The customers didn't mind him all snuggled up next to them as they sat on the couch letting the fire warm them.

I quickly stacked the coffee magazines and holiday-themed books along with a few nonfiction books about Honey Springs on the coffee table that I'd purchased from Crooked Cat Bookstore at the far end of the boardwalk.

I picked up the magazine with the fall decoration photo on the front and quickly flipped through it. I loved to get decoration ideas for the Bean Hive and my little log cabin.

"See anything you like in there?" Loretta Bebe asked in a singsong Southern drawl as she snuck up behind me.

"I do like how they arranged and stacked the different colors, shapes, and sizes of pumpkins on this front porch," I said and showed her the photo. "Thanks for the magazine drop-off."

"It's my pleasure. I like to flip through them and then spread the wealth." Loretta wiggled her brows. "And I brought some new ones that are already showcasing Thanksgiving. Can you believe it?"

Stacks of gold bangle bracelets rattled down on her wrist as she plunged her hand into her pocketbook and took out another pile of magazines.

"I wanted to make sure I dropped these off before we head down to Florida for a few weeks. We are going to see Elliot." She was referring to her son.

"That's so nice. How is he?" I asked and put the Halloween-themed magazine back on the coffee table before I took the stack I'd save to put out next month.

"You know, he's Elliot, but it's Birdie we are excited to see." Loretta smiled. She looked around. "Oh! Eleanor is here." There was excitement in her voice. She shoved her hot-pink painted nails into her short black hair, making it stand a little taller. "She's early," she said. "But if you want to get a few of those fancy pumpkins from that photo, you need to come to Hollow Manor. Eleanor has them."

She winked before she excused herself.

"She's a one-woman show," I muttered and picked up the poker to stoke the fire and then put another log on.

"Can I get you anything?" I asked several customers as I walked over to the coffee bar to make sure it was stocked as the morning rush continued.

All of them said they were fine, but I believed in making sure they were catered to. After all, this was my passion, not to mention my livelihood.

The coffee bar had six industrial thermoses with different blends of my specialty coffees as well as one filled with a decaffeinated blend. The coffee bar had everything you needed to take a coffee with you. Even an honor system where you could pay and go.

With it all cleaned and ready for the next round of pay-as-you-go customers, I made my way over to the opposite side where I had a tea bar for our tea-drinking customers.

We offered hot tea and cold tea with a nice selection of gourmet teas and loose-leaf teas. I loved having the antique tea pots from Wild and Whimsy Antique shop, which was also on the boardwalk. The pots were not just a decoration, but customers could enjoy their own pots by making them to their liking.

As I walked past another group, Eleanor's voice rang out, regaling them with her grand plans for the mansion's transformation. She painted a vivid picture of a place where the spooky reputation would be embraced, inviting them to experience the thrill of a magician's spell-binding tricks within its aged walls. The excitement in her voice was palpable, but beneath it all, a sense of unease gnawed at me.

Loretta stood next to her, offering approving head nods.

Glancing around the bustling coffee shop, I caught Bunny's critical scowl. Her silent disapproval spoke volumes, a reminder of the tensions that lingered between Eleanor and some of the townsfolk. Though the smiles, the chatter, and the aroma of steaming coffee filled the air, there was an unsettling feeling that something wasn't quite right.

I, too, had had my own encounter with the mansion. Something Patrick and I had never talked about since the one afternoon when we were seventeen and decided to see if the tales Eleanor had spun back then were true.

A shiver ran down my spine. The same shiver that'd happened all those years ago after Patrick and I took off running away from the old mansion.

Though I told Eleanor I'd cater the coffee for the big finale tonight, I still couldn't help but think about what secrets hid in the shadows of the mansion.

I couldn't shake the feeling that our cozy autumn haven was about to be thrust into a chilling journey where nothing would be as it seemed.

After all, I'd never stepped foot on the mansion grounds since I'd run away.

Little did I know that returning to Hollow Manor would awaken more than just memories.

Macchiato Murder is now available to purchase or in Kindle Unlimited.

RECIPES FROM THE BEAN HIVE

MAPLE BACON COFFEE

Ingredients:

6 strips bacon-for the syrup
1 cup pure maple syrup-for the syrup
1 cup whole milk
2 oz espresso
ground cinnamon, for garnish

Directions:

Make the maple bacon syrup:

1. You can bake the bacon at 425°F for 15–17 minutes, until crispy.

Or you can microwave the bacon or fry it. All of them are fine. I like to bake my bacon because I like it to bake evenly.

1. Transfer the bacon to a cutting board, blot with a paper towel to absorb any excess grease, and chop.
2. In a small saucepan add your chopped bacon and the maple syrup. Bring to a boil over medium-high heat, then reduce

the heat to low and simmer for 15 minutes, or until thickened slightly.

3. Remove the pot from the heat and let it sit for 15–20 minutes.
4. Strain the syrup and reserving the bacon bits for the later when you top the coffee.

Make the maple bacon latte:

1. Add milk to a milk frother and set to the steam setting. Steam until hot.

If you don't have a frother, you can warm the milk on the stove in a small saucepan over medium-low heat, stirring occasionally, until beginning to steam. Use a handheld immersion blender, blend on low speed until frothy.

1. In a coffee mug, stir together the espresso and 2 tablespoons of maple bacon syrup.
2. Pour in steamed milk until the mug is ¾ full, then top with foam.
3. Garnish with some of the bacon bits and a sprinkle of ground cinnamon.
4. Serve immediately. Enjoy!

HOT HONEY ALMOND MILK FLAT WHITE RECIPE

If you're looking for a delicious twist on your daily cup of coffee, try this hot honey almond milk flat white recipe.

Ingredients

1 shot espresso or strongly brewed coffee

2 teaspoons honey

½ cup almond milk

Cinnamon for garnish

Directions:

1. Add the espresso and honey to your desired mug and stir to combine.
2. 1 shot espresso,
3. 2 teaspoons honey
4. Froth the almond milk.
5. Pour frothed almond milk over the espresso,
6. garnish with a pinch of cinnamon

"APPALACHIAN SUMMER" BREAD

For the honeysuckle simple syrup:

1 1/2 cups fresh honeysuckle (Lonicera periclymenum) flowers

1 cup unbleached, non-GMO cane sugar

1 cup of filtered water

Bring 1 cup of water to boil in a small saucepan over medium-high heat. As soon as the water boils, add 1 cup of sugar and stir to dissolve. Turn heat off and add in honeysuckle flowers. Cover the saucepan with a lid and let this infuse while you move on to making the cake.

When you're ready for your honeysuckle simple syrup, strain the mixture through a fine-mesh sieve. Compost the honeysuckle flowers and reserve 1/3 cup of the syrup for your cake. Transfer any remaining syrup to a glass canning jar and store it in the refrigerator for 2-3 weeks. Use it to sweeten herbal teas, drizzle ice cream or other desserts, or to sweeten your summer botanical mixed drinks!

For the pound cake:

1 1/2 cups of unbleached all-purpose flour

1 teaspoon aluminum-free baking powder

1/4 teaspoon baking soda

1 teaspoon fine-ground sea salt

2 tablespoons of Honeysuckle Simple Syrup, plus 1/3 cup reserved

1/3 cup of buttermilk (or plain yogurt)

2 tablespoons of freshly grated organic lemon zest (or 18 drops of organic lemon essential oil)

1 cup of unbleached, non-GMO cane sugar

1/2 cup of avocado oil

2 eggs

Preheat the oven to 350 degrees. While the oven is heating, butter and flour a 9×5 loaf pan.

In a small bowl, combine flour, baking powder, baking soda, and salt. Gently whisk to combine, and set aside.

In a large bowl, combine sugar, oil, and lemon zest (or essential oil) and whisk until the mixture is smooth. Whisk in the eggs, one at a time, until combined. Finally, add buttermilk (or yogurt) and honeysuckle simple syrup, and gently whisk to combine.

Next, slowly incorporate the dry ingredients into the wet ingredients, whisking as you go to keep the batter smooth. Scrape down the sides of the bowl until everything is well incorporated.

Pour the batter into the prepared loaf pan, tapping the pan on the counter a few times to remove trapped air bubbles. Bake for 45-60 minutes, until a knife or toothpick comes out clean.

When the cake is finished baking, let it cool in the pan for 10 minutes before inverting it onto a cooling rack. Carefully turn the cake right-side up on the cooking rack and place a tray or dish underneath. Poke holes in the top of the cake (getting close to the cake edges) with a knife, skewer, or toothpick, and brush 1/3 cup of honeysuckle syrup over the cake. Feel free to reuse any syrup drippings caught in the tray under the cake.

Lastly, top the cake with a sugar glaze, and set it aside to allow time for the honeysuckle simple syrup to absorb, allow the glaze to slightly harden, and give the cake time to cool.

For the sugar glaze

1/3 cup of non-GMO powdered sugar
1-3 teaspoons of water

Add 1/3 cup of powdered sugar to a glass measuring cup and slowly drizzle a small amount of water into it, adding 1 teaspoon at a time and stirring with a spoon, until the mixture is smooth.

Drizzle the mixture back and forth over the top of the cake, allowing it to run down the sides.

BOOKS BY TONYA
SOUTHERN HOSPITALITY WITH A SMIDGEN OF HOMICIDE

Camper & Criminals Cozy Mystery Series

All is good in the camper-hood until a dead body shows up in the woods.

BEACHES, BUNGALOWS, AND BURGLARIES
DESERTS, DRIVING, & DERELICTS
FORESTS, FISHING, & FORGERY
CHRISTMAS, CRIMINALS, AND CAMPERS
MOTORHOMES, MAPS, & MURDER
CANYONS, CARAVANS, & CADAVERS
HITCHES, HIDEOUTS, & HOMICIDES
ASSAILANTS, ASPHALT & ALIBIS
VALLEYS, VEHICLES & VICTIMS
SUNSETS, SABBATICAL AND SCANDAL
TENTS, TRAILS AND TURMOIL
KICKBACKS, KAYAKS, AND KIDNAPPING
GEAR, GRILLS & GUNS
EGGNOG, EXTORTION, AND EVERGREEN
ROPES, RIDDLES, & ROBBERIES
PADDLERS, PROMISES & POISON
INSECTS, IVY, & INVESTIGATIONS
OUTDOORS, OARS, & OATH
WILDLIFE, WARRANTS, & WEAPONS
BLOSSOMS, BBQ, & BLACKMAIL
LANTERNS, LAKES, & LARCENY
JACKETS, JACK-O-LANTERN, & JUSTICE
SANTA, SUNRISES, & SUSPICIONS
VISTAS, VICES, & VALENTINES
ADVENTURE, ABDUCTION, & ARREST

RANGERS, RVS, & REVENGE
CAMPFIRES, COURAGE & CONVICTS
TRAPPING, TURKEY & THANKSGIVING
GIFTS, GLAMPING & GLOCKS
ZONING, ZEALOTS, & ZIPLINES
HAMMOCKS, HANDGUNS, & HEARSAY
QUESTIONS, QUARRELS, & QUANDARY
WITNESS, WOODS, & WEDDING
ELVES, EVERGREENS, & EVIDENCE
MOONLIGHT, MARSHMALLOWS, & MANSLAUGHTER
BONFIRE, BACKPACKS, & BRAWLS

Killer Coffee Cozy Mystery Series

Welcome to the Bean Hive Coffee Shop where the gossip is just as hot as the coffee.

SCENE OF THE GRIND
MOCHA AND MURDER
FRESHLY GROUND MURDER
COLD BLOODED BREW
DECAFFEINATED SCANDAL
A KILLER LATTE
HOLIDAY ROAST MORTEM
DEAD TO THE LAST DROP
A CHARMING BLEND NOVELLA (CROSSOVER WITH MAGICAL CURES MYSTERY)
FROTHY FOUL PLAY
SPOONFUL OF MURDER
BARISTA BUMP-OFF
CAPPUCCINO CRIMINAL
MACCHIATO MURDER
POUR-OVER PREDICAMENT
ICE COFFEE CORRUPTION

Holiday Cozy Mystery Series

CELEBRATE GOOD CRIMES!

FOUR LEAF FELONY
MOTHER'S DAY MURDER
A HALLOWEEN HOMICIDE
NEW YEAR NUISANCE
CHOCOLATE BUNNY BETRAYAL
FOURTH OF JULY FORGERY
SANTA CLAUSE SURPRISE
APRIL FOOL'S ALIBI

Kenni Lowry Mystery Series

Mysteries so delicious it'll make your mouth water and leave you hankerin' for more.

FIXIN' TO DIE
SOUTHERN FRIED
AX TO GRIND
SIX FEET UNDER
DEAD AS A DOORNAIL
TANGLED UP IN TINSEL
DIGGIN' UP DIRT
BLOWIN' UP A MURDER
HEAVENS TO BRIBERY

Magical Cures Mystery Series

Welcome to Whispering Falls where magic and mystery collide.

A CHARMING CRIME
A CHARMING CURE

A CHARMING POTION (novella)
A CHARMING WISH
A CHARMING SPELL
A CHARMING MAGIC
A CHARMING SECRET
A CHARMING CHRISTMAS (novella)
A CHARMING FATALITY
A CHARMING DEATH (novella)
A CHARMING GHOST
A CHARMING HEX
A CHARMING VOODOO
A CHARMING CORPSE
A CHARMING MISFORTUNE
A CHARMING BLEND (CROSSOVER WITH A KILLER COFFEE COZY)
A CHARMING DECEPTION

Mail Carrier Cozy Mystery Series

Welcome to Sugar Creek Gap where more than the mail is being delivered.

STAMPED OUT
ADDRESS FOR MURDER
ALL SHE WROTE
RETURN TO SENDER
FIRST CLASS KILLER
POST MORTEM
DEADLY DELIVERY
RED LETTER SLAY

Maisie Doss Mystery

SLEIGHT OF HAND

BOOKS BY TONYA

TANGLED LIES
GRAVE DECEPTION

About Tonya

Tonya has written over 100 novels, all of which have graced numerous bestseller lists, including the USA Today. *Best known for stories charged with emotion and humor and filled with flawed characters, her novels have garnered reader praise and glowing critical reviews. She lives with her husband and a very spoiled rescue cat named Ro. Tonya grew up in the small southern Kentucky town of Nicholasville. Now that her four boys are grown men, Tonya writes full-time in her camper she calls her SHAMPER (she-camper).*

Learn more about her be sure to check out her website tonyakappes.com. Find her on Facebook, Twitter, BookBub, and Instagram

Sign up to receive her newsletter, where you'll get free books, exclusive bonus content, and news of her releases and sales.

If you liked this book, please take a few minutes to leave a review now! Authors (Tonya included) really appreciate this, and it helps draw more readers to books they might like. Thanks!

This book is a work of fiction. The characters, incidents, and dialogue are drawn from the author's imagination and are not to be construed as real. Any resemblance to actual events or persons, living or dead, is entirely coincidental. *Cover artist: Mariah Sinclair: The Cover Vault. Editor Red Adept.*

www.ingramcontent.com/pod-product-compliance
Ingram Content Group UK Ltd.
Pitfield, Milton Keynes, MK11 3LW, UK
UKHW021650190726
13853UKWH00001B/181